*Endless
Treasure*

The World Publishing Company   *New York and Cleveland*

Endless Treasure

Unfamiliar
Tales
From
The Arabian
Nights

JOHN
HAMPDEN

Illustrated by
KURT WERTH

Published by The World Publishing Company
110 East 59th Street, New York, New York 10022
Library of Congress catalog card number: 70-101846
Text copyright © 1968 by John Hampden
Illustrations copyright © 1970 by Kurt Werth
Printed in the United States of America.
Designed by Jack Jaget

*For
Katherine
one day*

Contents

Introduction

EVEN before writing was invented, people must have loved telling stories and listening to them as they do in so many places today. In the East many men earned their living as storytellers. They took their stand wherever listeners would gather, at the corner of a bazaar (a street of shops), in the marketplace, in a great lord's hall or kitchen, or beside the campfire in the desert, surrounded by traveling merchants or wandering Arabs, with their camels and black tents. They told their stories from memory and no doubt they sometimes improved on them, hoping to get a few more coins afterwards. Stories were passed on by word of mouth, from father to son, from one storyteller to another, from one country or language to another, changing as they went.

So the tales in *The Arabian Nights* were passed on for centuries. Some came from India by way of Persia, one at least from Greece, and some perhaps from more distant countries. Nine hundred years ago the tales were translated into Arabic, and the people in them were turned into Arabs, living like the Arabs of the time; and later on they were written down, possibly in Cairo. Then, with other collections of stories, they were passed on from one copyist and reader to another.

By that time Arabic had become the language of millions of people, as it is today. The great prophet Mohammed, who founded the religion of Islam, had been born about A.D. 570, at Mecca in Arabia. He saw visions and heard voices, and he declared that there was only one God, Allah. He taught his followers, among other things, to pray to Allah every day, to give help to poor people, to fast on certain days, and to go as pilgrims to the ancient temple at Mecca. He formed the wandering tribes in the deserts of Arabia into one warlike nation. They set out to overcome all the peoples round about, and they and their successors, gathering armies as they went, conquered Persia, Central Asia, Western India, Palestine, Syria, and all northern Africa from Egypt to Morocco, and in A.D. 709 they crossed the Straits of Gibraltar to begin conquering Spain. They made Islam the religion of all these countries and Arabic their language, building beautiful mosques, temples for the worship of Allah. Meanwhile their merchants and missionaries had carried Islam farther still.

The Arabs, or Saracens as they were often called, were fierce, brave warriors, but where they came they made peace and set up a way of life more civilized than most of Europe was at that time. Their universities became great centers of learning, where literature and art, medicine, mathematics, astronomy and other sciences were studied, and Europe learned much from them. One of their most famous rulers was Haroun al-Rashid—on whom be peace, as the Moslems say of their dead. He ruled in Baghdad at the end of the eighth century, and he was not only a rich and powerful king but the Caliph, the religious head of Islam. After his death many legends gathered around his name.

The Arab countries were ruled by various kings, sultans, and emirs, and they chose wazirs (ministers) to help them in the business of government, with a grand wazir or chief minister. They and other rich men had many slaves, black, brown, and white, and sometimes several wives. They lived, when they could afford it, in such splendid houses as those described in *The Arabian Nights*, houses with marble pillars and rich carpets and courtyards full of tinkling fountains and sweetly scented flowers.

The tales had been circulated in Arabic for some hundreds of years before they were known in the West. Then Antoine Galland translated them into French in 1704 and they quickly became popular all over Europe. An English translation from the French, not a good one, very soon appeared, and the stories became firm favorites with readers young and old. Since then there have been several translations from Arabic into English; they are named in the Acknowledgments in this book.

In complete translations of the tales they are all linked together; they are told to the King, her husband, by the Princess Shahrazad, and that is a fairy tale in itself. Soon after the King's first marriage he found that his Queen was deceiving him wickedly. He had her executed at once, and swore that no wife should ever deceive him again. So he ordered his Grand Wazir to bring him every day the most beautiful girl that could be found. He married her at once, and next day he had her executed. This cruelty went on until the Wazir could not find another suitable girl; then the Wazir's own daughter, the beautiful Shahrazad, insisted that she herself would go to the King. Her head was full of wonderful tales. That night she began to tell the King one of these tales, and she took care to reach the most exciting point just as morning came and the King had to get up. He could not bear to miss the rest, so he said she could live for another day. The next night she played the same trick, and so it went on and on, till the King was so fond of her that he would not have her killed. So in Arabic the book is called *The Thousand Nights and One Night*.

Some of the best of the Princess's stories are in this book; not the stories which everyone knows already, such as "Aladdin," "Sinbad," and "Ali Baba," but stories which have been told for young readers rarely, if ever, before.

1969

J.H.

Acknowledgments

The stories in this book are based on the following translations:

The Arabian Nights Entertainments, translated by Edward William Lane, edited by Edward Stanley Poole, 3 vols., London, 1859.

The Arabian Nights Entertainments, translated by Jonathan Scott, edited by G. F. Townsend. Revised edition, 1 vol., London, n.d. [1866].

The Book of the Thousand Nights and a Night, translated by Richard F. Burton, 10 vols., Benares, 1885.

The Book of the Thousand Nights and One Night, rendered into English from the literal and complete French translation of Dr. J. C. Mardrus by Powys Mathers, The Folio Society, London, 4 vols, 1958. A few stories have been based on this by courteous permission of Routledge and Kegan Paul Ltd., London, the original publishers of this (still copyright) translation, and Dover Publications, Inc., New York, have courteously agreed.

Grateful acknowledgments are due also to four librarians, Mrs. Diane Crook, Mrs. Mandy Powys, Mrs. Sandra Morgan, and Mrs. Glenys Carr; and to my wife, Rosalind Vallance, for much help and advice.

1969

J.H.

*Endless
Treasure*

Endless
Treasure

THE great and famous Caliph of Baghdad, Haroun al-Rashid, on whom be peace, had one great fault; he often boasted that no man alive gave such splendid gifts as he did. This worried his chief minister, the Grand Wazir Jafar, until one day he plucked up enough courage to speak of it.

After kissing the ground three times at the Caliph's feet, he said, "O Commander of the Faithful, forgive your humble slave Jafar that he dares to lift his voice in your presence, to say that the true believer is always humble before Allah, and never boasts of his riches. It would be more noble of you, O Caliph, to leave it to your subjects to praise you for giving splendid gifts. You are not the greatest giver. There is a young man in the city of Basra who gives richer gifts than the most powerful king can give."

The Caliph went very red in the face and his eyes flamed with fury. "Miserable dog of a Wazir," he roared, "do you know that to tell me such a lie means death?"

"I speak nothing but truth," answered Jafar, prostrating

himself. "When I was last in Basra I was the guest of this young man, Abu al-Kasim, and I was astonished. He is certainly the most generous giver of our time. He must have endless treasure. If you do not believe me, O Caliph, send a messenger to test my words."

Haroun al-Rashid was so furious that he could not speak.

He signed to his guards, who laid hold of Jafar and took him to prison. The Caliph stalked out of the room and went straight to the apartments of his Queen, Zobeide, where he flung himself down on a sofa without a word.

She went pale when she saw him so angry, and she was too wise to ask him what was wrong. She brought him a goblet of rose-scented water and said, "The blessing of Allah be on you. Some days are black and some are white. May all your days be white with happiness, my lord."

Her sweet voice calmed him, as it always did. He drank the rose water slowly and then he told her everything.

Zobeide saw that Jafar's life was in great danger. She did not dare to defend him, but she did say that a messenger sent to Basra could easily find out whether there was any truth in what he had said.

"That is only just," said the Caliph. "He has been a faithful servant. I will not hang him till I know. But there is no one I can trust. I will go to Basra myself, in disguise."

Nothing the Queen could say would alter his mind, and that very day he set out from Baghdad alone, dressed as a traveling merchant and riding a camel. Allah took him safely to Basra, where he alighted at the chief khan, the best inn in the city.

Without even waiting to wash and eat first, Haroun said to the doorkeeper, "Is it true that there is in this city a young man named Abu al-Kasim who is a more splendid giver of gifts than any king?"

"Indeed he is," said the doorkeeper. "The blessings of Allah be on him! If I had a hundred mouths and a hundred tongues in every mouth I could not praise his generosity as it ought to be praised."

Haroun snorted, and went to his supper and his bed, after seeing his camel cared for. Next morning he set out on foot, and asked a shopkeeper in the bazaar the way to Abu's house.

"If you do not know that," said the man, "you must have come from far. Abu al-Kasim is better known in Basra than any king in his own city. I will lend you my boy to guide you."

When the Caliph reached Abu al-Kasim's abode he found that it was a splendid palace, beautifully built of marble, with great doors of green jade. A number of boy slaves were playing in the courtyard, and he said to one of them, "Go, tell your master that a stranger is here who has come from Baghdad especially to see him."

The boy guessed that the stranger was no common man, although not richly dressed, and he ran to tell his master. Abu came down into the courtyard at once to welcome the unexpected visitor, and when they had greeted each other in the name of Allah, Abu took him by the hand and led him into a hall of strange beauty. They seated themselves on a soft couch of green silk, embroidered with gold, which ran around four sides of the hall. Abu clapped his hands and twelve white slaves entered, carrying cups of agate and rock crystal, set outside with rubies and filled with the finest red wine. They were followed by twelve girls, each of them as beautiful as the full moon in a cloudless sky, bearing porcelain basins of fruit and flowers, and large golden goblets of sherbet made with snow. When the Caliph had tried them all he said to himself, "I have never tasted anything so delicious, although the finest food and drink in the eastern world are brought daily to my palace."

Now Abu led him to a second chamber, even more splendid than the first, where they were served with fish and chicken and meat on golden dishes. Then they went into a third chamber, where light pastries and jam and honey and wonderful jellies were served, followed by white wines and red wines in goblets of gold, while sweet singers and wonderful musicians entertained them. "This," said the Caliph to himself, "is such a meal and such a concert as I could hardly have expected on earth."

Abu, with polite excuses, left the hall for a moment and returned carrying a wand of amber in one hand and in the other a little tree of silver, which bore emeralds as leaves and rubies as fruit. He set the tree in front of the Caliph, who saw that there was a golden peacock of rare workmanship perched on the top of it. Abu touched the bird with the wand, and at once it stretched its golden wings, spread the jeweled splendor of its tail, and began to turn quickly on itself, sending out little jets of perfume which filled the hall with delicious scent.

But no sooner had the Caliph settled down to watch this wonder than Abu carried it off. "This is strange behavior," said Haroun angrily to himself, "snatching it away in that fashion. It doesn't look as though Abu understands how to be generous. He must have thought I would ask for the bird."

Abu al-Kasim came back leading a little boy who was as beautiful as sunlight and was dressed in gold brocade sewn all over with pearls. He carried a cup carved from a single giant ruby and filled with purple wine. He kissed the earth between the Caliph's hands and gave him the cup. Haroun drank all the wine, which was the finest he had ever tasted, and handed back the cup. As he did so, to his astonishment it filled itself with wine. Haroun emptied it again, and again it filled itself at once.

He could not help saying to his host, "How does this marvel happen?"

"The cup was made by a wise and holy man who knew all the secrets of nature," replied Abu al-Kasim. He took the child by the hand and hurried him away.

"By the life of my head," said Haroun angrily to himself, "either this young man has gone mad or he has no idea of good manners. As soon as he sees that I am pleased with anything he snatches it away. When I get back I will teach Jafar to be a better judge of men, and to turn his tongue around his mouth before he speaks."

But at this point he forgot the tree, the peacock, and the cup completely, for Abu al-Kasim came back bringing a little girl, dressed in diamonds and so wonderfully beautiful that Haroun could not think of anything but her beauty. He sat spellbound while she played, on the ivory lute which she carried, such music as no one could expect to hear except in Paradise.

When she ended he cried to his host, "O youth, how you are to be envied!"—at which Abu took the little girl's hand and ran with her out of the hall.

This third insult was too much for the Caliph. He knew

he would lose his temper if he stayed any longer, so when his host came back he rose and said, "O Abu al-Kasim, I am overcome by the generosity with which you have received me, an unknown stranger. Allow me now to retire, to leave you to your rest, for I must not trespass further on your kindness."

The young man bowed, not wishing to detain his guest,

and led him to the palace gate, where he said, "I beg you to forgive me for having given you entertainment unworthy of so delightful a visitor."

So they saluted each other, and the Caliph walked back to his khan, muttering furiously to himself, "That young fool did nothing but show off his riches and treasures to me. Generous, indeed! I'll teach Jafar what happens to anyone who lies to me!"

He was still fuming when he reached the gate of the khan. There he found waiting for him a crescent-line of young slaves, half of them black, half of them white. In the middle stood the little lute girl from Abu al-Kasim's palace. On her right stood the little boy carrying the magic ruby cup, and on her left another little boy holding the silver tree with the peacock perched on it. As the Caliph came through the gateway all the slaves prostrated themselves and the little girl came forward. Kneeling to the Caliph she presented to him, on a brocaded cushion, a scroll of silk paper.

He took it, unrolled it, and read these words: "The peace of Allah be upon a charming guest, whose coming brought happiness. O best of companions, it seemed to me that you were not displeased by these things which I now venture to put before you; the tree, the wine cup, and the lute. I hope that you will accept them in homage from one whose house you have honored—Abu al-Kasim."

"By the honor of my ancestors," cried Haroun, "how I have misunderstood this young man! Where is my generosity now? It is nothing compared with his! O faithful Jafar, how right you were to rebuke me for my pride and boasting!"

He called for pen and ink and the finest silk paper, to write his thanks to Abu al-Kasim, and sent the scroll by one of the slaves. The others went back with him to Baghdad.

The first thing he did was to release Jafar from his dungeon and give him a rich robe of honor, to show the whole court that he was again the Grand Wazir. Then he told Jafar the story of his adventures, and said to him, "What can I do to reward Abu al-Kasim?"

"O Commander of the Faithful," answered Jafar. "It is clear from what you say that this young man lives and behaves like a king, and is much loved in his city. You might make him King of Basra."

"O wise old man," cried Haroun. "Let the patent of royalty be drawn up at once for me to sign. Then do you take it to him yourself and bring him here, so that he can be crowned in my presence and we can rejoice together."

All this was done, and the great Caliph boasted no more of the splendid gifts he gave. He spread through Baghdad the tale of Abu al-Kasim's generosity.

The
Black
Monkey

ABU MOHAMMED was the son of a barber who died and left nothing to his widow and son because he had nothing to leave. They were very poor, but this made no difference to Abu. He was far too lazy to work. He was so lazy that he would not brush a fly off his nose when it stung him, or move into the shade when the sun began to scorch him. Everyone called him Abu Lazybones, but he did not care. His poor mother went out to work and earned just enough to buy rice for them both, and Abu went on sleeping away his days.

One day his mother came to him and said, "Here are five silver dinars which I have saved from many months of work. Take these, my son, to the Sheikh Mustapha, for he is setting out very soon on a trading voyage to China. He is a very kind man. If you ask him, perhaps he will buy goods for you in China and bring them home so that you can sell them at a profit."

Abu opened one eye and looked at her, but he did not move.

This was too much for his mother. "Abu," she said, "if you do not get up and take these dinars to Sheikh Mustapha, I will bring you nothing to eat and nothing to drink. I will not come near you again. You will starve."

Abu opened both eyes and looked at her, and he saw that she meant it.

"Help me to sit up," he said, and she did so.

"Now bring me my shoes," he said, and she brought them.

"Put them on, Mother." She put them on.

"Now lift me onto my feet." She did so.

"Hold me up, so that I can walk." She put her arm around him and helped him down the street toward the river. He went very slowly, stumbling over the skirts of his dress.

When they reached the river his mother said, "There is the Sheikh. Go to him."

She gave Abu a push and he stumbled forward by himself. He saluted the Sheikh and said, "O Sheikh Mustapha, I am Abu Mohammed. My mother, who is a poor widow, has sent me to ask, in the name of Allah, if you will take these five dinars to buy goods for me in the land of China, in the hope that I can sell them at a profit. I beg you, my lord, to do us this kindness."

"In the name of Allah, I will do it," said the Sheikh, taking the money, and Abu went back to his mother.

Next day Mustapha with a company of other merchants set sail for China, where they arrived without accident. When they had bought and sold as they wished, the ship set

out on the voyage home, but when they had been three days
at sea the Sheikh suddenly smote his forehead and cried, "We
must go back!"

"Why?" asked the other merchants. "What is wrong?"

"I promised Abu Mohammed, in the name of Allah, that
I would buy goods for him in China, and I forgot it. I must
go back."

The other merchants would not agree to this, but they did
agree that Abu must have his profit, so they collected twenty
silver dinars among themselves and Mustapha took this gladly.

Presently they called at an island where there was a large
city. The merchants went ashore, and bought precious metals
and precious stones, spices and silks. Mustapha came to one
shop in the bazaar which sold animals and there among others
were a dozen monkeys tethered by chains, all of them brown
except one, which was black. The others bit and tormented
the black monkey whenever their owner was not looking,
and Mustapha was sorry for it. He said to the shopkeeper,
"I have with me five silver dinars, belonging to a poor father-
less boy. Will you sell the black monkey for that?"

"It is a bargain for you," said the man, "but I will." So
Mustapha's servants carried the monkey on board the ship
and tied it to the mast.

Soon afterward the ship came to another island and cast
anchor. Here there were great beds of oysters containing
pearls on the bottom of the sea, and divers offering themselves for hire. The merchants hired several, who were soon
bringing up very fine pearls.

When the monkey saw this it broke its chain and leaped

overboard. "There is no majesty and no might save in Allah," said Mustapha. "I am afraid that the monkey is lost to us, with the luck of poor Abu, for whom I bought it."

But a few minutes later the monkey climbed on board, with both its hands and its mouth full of the finest pearls, which it laid down at Mustapha's feet. The Sheikh marveled at this, saying, "There is much mystery in this monkey. And all these precious pearls are for Abu."

Soon they sailed on to a third island, but here all the people were savages who ate men. They attacked the ship in their canoes, and carried off all the crew and the merchants. That night they killed and ate some of them. Mustapha and the merchants they tied up with strong ropes and threw into a hut, to be eaten later.

As soon as it was dark the prisoners struggled to free themselves from the ropes, but it was no use; in the end they gave themselves up for lost, feeling sure they would be killed and eaten next day, and fell to their prayers. Then a strange thing happened. The monkey crept silently into the hut and set them all free, untying the ropes or biting through them with its strong teeth. They stole away silently through the darkness to their ship, hoisted sail as quietly as they could, and were out of sight before daylight came.

"I owe my life to Abu's monkey," said Mustapha. "I shall give him a thousand silver dinars as a reward."

"It is just," said the rest of the merchants, and all did the same. Mustapha kept all the money for Abu.

They had no more adventures after this and soon reached their own city, where Mustapha sent word to Abu Lazy-

bones. He was asleep as usual, but his mother got the message and went to him. "Wake up," she said. "The Sheikh Mustapha has come back and is asking for you. If it is the will of Allah, this is good fortune for you. You must go to the Sheikh at once."

"Lift me up," said Abu, and his mother lifted him on to his feet.

"Now help me to walk," he said, stumbling over the skirts of his robe. She helped him to walk to the riverbank, where he found Mustapha, with the monkey on a chain.

"Allah has prospered you," he said to Abu. "Take this monkey and lead it home. I will come to you there tomorrow."

Then he went to the bazaar, where he sold his merchandise, and because the pearls which the monkey had gathered were of the very finest quality he sold them for twenty thousand gold dinars.

Next morning he went to Abu's house with two slaves carrying all the bags of gold and silver dinars, at which Abu was so astonished that he got up by himself and kissed the hem of Mustapha's robe, thanking him again and again.

When they had rejoiced together Abu's mother said, "By the mercy of Allah you are now well off. Wake up. Take a shop in the bazaar, stock it with the finest goods, and buy and sell so that we shall never be hungry again."

Abu got up and shook himself; he did what his mother had said. Every day he sat on the divan in his shop, buying and selling, while half the day the monkey sat beside him, eating and drinking with him. Many people came to the shop to see this strange sight. But every day the monkey went away from ten o'clock until twelve o'clock and then came back with a bag containing a thousand gold dinars which it gave to Abu, who was soon very rich.

This went on for months, until one evening Abu was sitting in the garden of his beautiful house when the monkey came to him and, for the first time, spoke.

"O Abu," said the monkey, "I ask you to do one thing for me. Find a white cock and bring it to me here in the garden."

Abu was very frightened, but he said, "I hear and I obey," and it was not long before he came running back, carrying a white cock. The monkey was holding a snake which it set down in front of the cock.

At once the two began to fight and they went on fighting until the cock had killed the snake. Then it ate the snake. Then the monkey killed the cock, pulled out all its long feathers and stuck them into the earth, one by one and far apart. It stood in front of each feather in turn, making strange clicking noises with its tongue. After that it went to Abu, bowed to him politely, and leaped into the air so high that it vanished from sight.

At that all the feathers grew swiftly into tall trees of pure gold, with emeralds for leaves and rubies and pearls for fruit, making for Abu the most valuable orchard that ever a man had. But the monkey was never seen again.

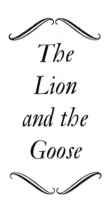

The
Lion
and the
Goose

THERE was once a beautiful young goose who lived all by herself on the edge of a wood. She knew nothing of the great world, but she was very happy. There were delicious herbs and grasses for her to eat, the brook brought her clear water to drink, and the sun shone.

Then one night she had a terrible dream. A strange, tall creature such as she had never seen before appeared to her, walking on its hind legs, and the creature said, "I am Man, the Son of Adam. Come to me, little goose, come and let me stroke your soft feathers. They are so beautiful."

Very pleased by this flattery, the young goose got up, but at that moment, in her dream, there was a great peal of thunder and a deep voice cried, "Beware the Son of Adam, beware! Today he will make friends with you; tomorrow he will kill you and eat you. He is the most cunning of creatures. He brings down the birds of the air with pellets of clay, he hauls fishes in his nets from the depths of the sea, and with his wiles he can master the most powerful of beasts. Beware the Son of Adam, beware, beware!"

The goose awoke, shaking with fear, afraid to move. Even when day came she hid herself among the bushes until she was so hungry that she had to go out to look for food. Presently she came to a cave, in front of which stood a handsome young lion, who greeted her kindly.

"Who are you?" said Lion.

"I am Goose, of the bird people," she answered, "and who, sir, are you?"

"I am Lion, the son of the Sultan, the King of Beasts. But why are you looking so frightened? I will not hurt you, beautiful goose."

Then she told him her dream, at which he lashed his tail in fury and roared until the hills re-echoed. "This my father has told me," he growled. "All the creatures of the earth go in danger so long as the Son of Adam lives."

"O my lord Prince," said Goose, "our only hope is in you. You are so brave and strong. Seek out the Son of Adam and kill him! I beg you, kill him before he kills us all!"

"That I must and will do!" roared Lion. "Cunning as he is, I will master him!" And at once he set out, with Goose walking beside him.

Soon they came to a road, which they followed, and presently they saw a cloud of dust coming along the road. Then a creature galloped out of the dust, panting and braying.

"Stop!" said Lion. "Who are you and why are you running so fast?"

"O Prince of Beasts," he answered, stopping and bowing

his head in homage. "I am Ass, of the animal people, and I am fleeing from the Son of Adam."

"Ur-rh," growled Lion. "Are you afraid that the Son of Adam will kill you?"

"Not so, O Prince," answered Ass, "but he makes me his slave. He puts a thing called saddle on my back, and binds it there with things called girths, which he tightens under my belly. He thrusts a thing called bit into my mouth, fastened with leather thongs, he climbs onto my back and stabs me with a thing called goad to make me carry him wherever he wants to go. This will go on year after year, until I am too old to carry him further. Then he will sell me to the water carrier, who will hang heavy skins of water across my back and make me work until I die. Can any grief be greater than this? Woe is me, woe is me."

Goose shivered with fear at Ass's story, and Lion roared again in his anger. "Where are you going?" he asked.

"I shall go on," answered Ass, "until I find a place where the Son of Adam cannot find me. But look!" Another cloud of dust had appeared on the road, and at sight of it Ass brayed in terror, flung up his heels, and galloped away as fast as he could go.

"This may be the Son of Adam," growled Lion, sharpening his terrible claws on the hard ground. Goose hid behind a bush, and they waited.

Out of the dust cloud there came a handsome black horse, with a blaze on his forehead like a bright silver coin. Neighing loudly he came to a halt before Lion and gracefully bent his head in greeting.

"O majestic beast," said Lion, "who are you and why are you fleeing so fast into this wilderness?"

"O Prince," he replied, "I am Horse, of the animal people, and I am fleeing from the Son of Adam."

"Are you not ashamed?" asked Lion. "A splendid creature, so large, so strong, so swift of foot as you are! Could you not kill him with a single kick from one of your hoofs? Why do you run away?"

"Because I am no match for him, O Prince. He masters me with his cunning ways. He hobbles me with ropes made of palm fibers, to keep me from getting away. He makes my head fast to a high peg, so that I can neither kneel nor lie down. He binds a saddle on my back, he thrusts an iron bit into my mouth and pulls at it so cruelly with leather thongs called reins that when he is mounted on my back he forces me to go wherever he wishes. When I grow too old to carry him swiftly he will sell me to the miller, who will blindfold me and compel me to walk around and around in a circle, working his mill, until one day I fall dead. Can you wonder that I flee from the Son of Adam?"

Goose shivered with fear, and Lion lashed his tail in fury. At that moment they saw another cloud of dust approaching them along the road, and Horse looked at it in horror.

"That must be the Son of Adam," he neighed. "But he shall not make me prisoner again!" Then with a great flurry of thudding hoofs he galloped away.

Out of the dust cloud came a strange and angry gurgling noise.

"This must be the Son of Adam," growled Lion. "I will tear him to pieces!"

He crouched like a cat, gathering himself together to spring, but at that moment a tawny head appeared above the dust, and they saw that it was a camel.

The great beast came to a halt when he reached them, and stopped his angry gurgling.

"Greeting, O Son of the Sultan," he said. "Greeting, my fair young goose."

"Greeting, O Camel," they replied, and Lion growled, "Why do you gallop so fast? Are you too fleeing from the Son of Adam?"

"I am indeed," answered Camel. "All creatures must flee from him who hope to escape his wiles."

"But you are so large and strong," growled Lion. "Are you not a match for him?"

"No," answered Camel. "He is too clever. No one can defeat him except Death. He puts through my nostrils a string made of goat's hair, which he calls nose ring, and over my head a thing he calls halter, which grips me by the throat. They make me so helpless that the smallest of his children can lead me. Then he loads me with heavy burdens, and makes me carry these burdens for him far across the desert. He works me day and night until I am too worn out to be of use to him any more; then he will take me to the butcher, who will kill me so that he can sell my hide to the tanners to make leather and my flesh to the cooks to make food for believers in Allah. There is no hope for me unless I can escape."

"When did you leave the Son of Adam?" asked Lion.

"At sunset yesterday," answered Camel. "I have galloped all night and all today, and I am very weary, but I dare not stop until I have found a hiding place where the Son of Adam cannot find me. I am sure he is following me."

"Wait," said Lion, "wait here until he comes, then you can watch me tear him to pieces, and you will know that you are free."

"No, I dare not," answered Camel. "Let me go, O Son of the Sultan of Beasts. The Son of Adam may be too clever even for you. And look, he is coming now!"

Another cloud of dust had appeared on the long white road. Camel looked at it for a moment, then turned and galloped away toward the distant trees.

Again Lion crouched, getting ready to spring, but this time the cloud of dust came on very slowly, and it was a very small cloud. When at last it reached Lion and Goose, there came out of it the funniest little creature they had ever seen. He was like an old monkey, with a very wrinkled face, and he walked, or rather staggered along, on his hind legs, carrying on one shoulder a basket of tools and on the other shoulder a dozen planks of wood.

Lion went to meet him and said, "Greetings, little creature, who are you and why do you come this way?"

"O Prince of Beasts," he answered. "May the blessing of Allah be upon you! I am Carpenter, of the carpenter people, and—and—" he burst into tears "—I am fleeing from the Son of Adam, who is my enemy." He stood there with the tears running down his face, looking sillier than ever.

"It is right for you to fear the Son of Adam," said Lion, "since you are such a feeble creature. But where are you going and why are you carrying that wood?"

"O Prince," replied Carpenter, "your royal father's Wazir, my lord Leopard, has sent for me to make him a strong fort which will protect him against his enemy, the Son of Adam. I am on my way to the Wazir now."

"It is not right," snorted Lion, "that Leopard should have a fort when I have none. You must make me a fort with that wood, here and now."

"No," said Carpenter. "I dare not. When my lord Leopard heard of it he would kill me."

"What!" roared Lion. "Will you disobey me!" He gave Carpenter a pat with his paw. It was a gentle pat, but Carpenter fell flat on his back in the dust, with his tools and planks on top of him. Lion laughed and laughed, because Carpenter looked so silly, and even Goose laughed a little. Carpenter was very angry, but he was afraid of Lion so he pretended to smile as he staggered to his feet, dusting himself down.

"Now," said Lion, "will you build me a fort?"

"I will, your Royal Highness," replied Carpenter.

He set to work at once with saw and hammer and nails, and soon made a little house with small round holes for windows and a small door. Then he turned to Lion and bowed low.

"It is small," said Lion, walking around it and looking at it doubtfully.

"But very strong," said Carpenter. "Will your Highness deign to enter, to see how well it fits?" He picked up his hammer and some of his largest nails.

Lion squeezed himself through the narrow doorway, but

the house was so small that his tail was left outside. Carpenter twisted the tail and jammed it into the box. He slammed the door and with a dozen hammer blows he had nailed it fast.

There came a muffled roar from Lion. "Let me out, Carpenter, let me out, or it will be the worse for you!"

"Not I!" cried Carpenter, dancing with joy. "Make fun of me, would you? Knock me down, would you? Laugh at me, would you? I am Man, the Son of Adam! I have the last laugh!"

He picked up his longest chisel and through one of the holes he stabbed Lion to death.

Then he shouldered his bag of tools and went back the way he had come, singing to himself as he went. But Goose never stopped running until she was safe home again in her friendly wood.

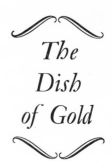

The
Dish
of Gold

THERE was once a merchant who spent his money so rashly that in time he had nothing left except debts, and fear made him almost mad. He left his wife and children and his native city, and wandered about the world, begging his way from place to place and hardly knowing where he went.

At last he came to a great city and passed through the gate into the main street. There he saw a company of men, richly dressed, going along together, so he followed behind them. Presently they went through a marble doorway into a splendid palace. He went with them, and they led him into a great hall, where they bowed low before a man who looked like a prince, for he was seated on a golden chair and servants in splendid liveries stood about him.

Then the man was afraid, for he was in rags and he had no right to be there. He feared for his life. He went quickly to a dim corner of the great hall, and sat down on the marble floor to rest, relieved that no one took any notice of him.

After a time a servant came in, leading four hunting dogs

which wore collars of gold, and tied them up with chains of silver in the same corner of the hall. Then he set in front of each dog a large golden dish full of the choicest meats and went away.

The poor man watched the dogs enviously as they began to eat, for he was starving, and presently one of the dogs looked up at him and saw the hunger in his face. The dog drew back from the dish and signed with his paw to the man

to come and eat, which he did eagerly. When he had emptied the dish he put it down on the floor but the dog pushed it toward him, clearly meaning him to take it. He picked it up and, hiding it under his rags, he stole out of the hall, feeling like a thief.

He journeyed on until he came to a town, where he sold the dish for a thousand ducats of gold. Then he went back to his native city, paid all his debts, and set up in business again. This time he prospered, for he had learned wisdom, so that he became richer and richer as the years went by. But the thought of the dish of gold weighed on his mind until he could bear it no longer. He put a thousand ducats of gold and a bag of jewels into a purse and set out for that great city, riding on a fine camel with ten richly dressed servants to attend him.

When they came to the city he found it sadly changed. The walls were in ruins; the great iron gates had fallen from their hinges; the main street was empty except for a few starving dogs sniffing along the gutters.

Dismounting and leaving his camel with a servant, he went alone up the street until he came to the palace in which the dog had given him the golden dish.

That too was in ruins. The walls were shattered, the roof had fallen in, there was only dirt and refuse on the floors which had once been spread with splendid carpets. There was no one there except an old man, pale and haggard, who was sitting on the broken steps of the main doorway.

"Ho, there!" cried the merchant. "What has brought ruin on the city? What have time and fortune done with the lord of this palace?"

"I was the lord of it," answered the old man. "I built it, and lived in it like a sultan, until time took away from me everything that I had. But who are you, and why do you ask?"

Then the merchant told his story, and afterwards he said, "I have here with me a thousand ducats of gold, which is the price I got for the dish, and a gift of precious stones. I owe everything to that dish, which was rightly yours. I beg you to accept these from me, so that I may pay my debt."

The old man rose to his feet, and now he looked as princely as he had done when the merchant had seen him first. "My friend," he answered, "I thank you with all my heart. But can I be so mean as to take back the price of a gift which a dog of mine generously gave you? Never!"

He turned and went slowly away.

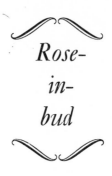

Rose-
in-
bud

LONG, long ago there was a Sultan whose chief minister, the Grand Wazir, had a daughter who was famous for her great beauty and her goodness of heart. Her name was Rose-in-bud.

One day it pleased the Sultan to call together all his nobles and courtiers for a great ball game. It was played on a field beside the Wazir's palace, so Rose-in-bud sat at her own window to watch. The Sultan sat on a chair of state beside the field, under a canopy of scarlet silk, with his guards around him. Rose-in-bud looked idly at the guards, and then took a deep breath. There was a young man among them whom she did not know, whom she felt at first glance to be the most wonderful young man she had ever seen.

She turned to one of her ladies-in-waiting. "What is the name of that handsome young man among the guards?" she asked.

"Oh, my lady," said the girl, "they are all handsome; they are such fine fellows. Which one do you mean?"

"Wait till the end of the game," she answered. "He will have to pass under this window, and then I can point him out to you."

She did more. When at last the young man rode past under the window she took an apple and dropped it in front of him. Startled, he looked up. Their eyes met, and in that instant they lost their hearts to each other. "His name is Ans al-Wujud," whispered the girl beside her, as he rode away.

"Can you keep a secret?" Rose-in-bud asked.

"Oh, my lady, indeed I can. Any secret of yours is safe with me."

Rose-in-bud went to her chamber, where she wrote a letter to Ans. She folded it in a piece of embroidered silk and asked the lady to take it to Captain Ans and bring his reply. He read the letter with great joy and wrote an answer which the lady took at once to her mistress. Rose-in-bud kissed it joyfully, touched her forehead with it, and read it three times before she wrote a reply, which again she gave to the lady to take to Ans.

But this time things went badly. On her way the lady met a chamberlain who said to her, "Where are you going in such a hurry?"

She stammered something and went on, but in her confusion she dropped the letter, which was picked up at once by one of the Wazir's servants, who took it to his master.

The Wazir read it with horror and showed it to his wife. "This will never do," she cried.

He tugged at his beard, and groaned, and said, "How angry the Sultan would be if he heard of it! Ans is such a favorite

of his that he plans to marry him to a princess at least. If Ans tried to marry Rose-in-bud it would ruin us all. The Sultan is terrible when he is angry. We must send her away at once to a place where Ans can never find her. But where is there such a place?"

The Wazir's wife, who had been weeping, dried her tears and said, "There is a place which you seem to have forgotten. In the midst of the Sea of Treasures there is an island called the Mountain of the Mother, and on the mountain in that island stands a strong castle in which no man lives. Send her there, O my husband, with servants and guards, and we shall be saved from this great danger."

"She shall go tonight," said the Wazir, and called for his most trusted servants.

Meanwhile the messenger had gone, weeping and wringing her hands, to tell Rose-in-bud that she had lost the letter. Rose-in-bud was very much afraid, and when her father came at nightfall and told her she must get ready at once to make a long journey, she guessed what was happening. She begged her father not to send her away, but he hardened his heart because he was so much afraid of the Sultan, who could be very cruel. There was nothing else for it; Rose-in-bud must go. But before she went she managed to send off another letter to her lover to tell him she was going—she did not know where.

The caravan gathered by torchlight in the Wazir's courtyard—servants and guards, camels, horses and baggage mules, and litters for Rose-in-bud and her ladies. She said goodbye tearfully to her father and mother, and got into her litter with one of her ladies, who drew the curtains close. Then they all set out.

After some days' travel across the desert they came to a forest by the shore of the Sea of Treasures. There they built a ship which carried them to the Mountain of the Mother, in the midst of the sea. There they found a splendid castle with no sign of life in it except the mice which scuttled away when they went in. Some of the servants sailed back in the ship, which they burned when they reached the shore, and then they went back to the Wazir.

The morning after they had left, Ans rose early. He prayed the dawn prayer to Allah, and was getting ready to wait upon the Sultan when a servant brought him Rose-in-bud's last letter. When he read it the shock was so great that he fell unconscious, and when he recovered he was beside himself. He made up his mind to seek Rose-in-bud throughout the world until he found her. So that night he took off his fine silk clothes, put on the poor rough robes of a fakir, a holy beggar, and wandered out into the darkness, not knowing or caring where he went.

For months he journeyed on, suffering much from thirst and hunger and the fierce heat of the sun, asking everyone he met for news of the caravan, or of Rose-in-bud, and learning nothing.

Presently he came to a forest, where he rested in the shade, and found figs to eat, and fresh water. He went on wearily through the forest, when suddenly a great lion leaped into his path with a terrible roar, and crouched growling as though about to spring upon him. Ans gave himself up for lost. He prostrated himself, saying, "There is no might save in Allah, the Compassionate, the Merciful."

Then he remembered having read in books that a lion can often be flattered into being friendly, so he said, "O noble lion, O Sultan of Beasts, O lord of forest and desert, O mighty and terrible Leo, have pity on me. I am a lover, seeking only for news of my lady, Rose-in-bud, because my heart will break if I cannot find her. Help me, great Sultan!"

The lion growled no more. It came forward and gently licked his hands, and then beckoning him with one paw to follow, it trotted away between the trees. It led him into the desert and stopped where a long line of hoofprints in the sand showed that a large caravan of camels and horses had passed. The lion pointed the way they had gone.

"O noble Sultan," cried Ans, "I thank you with all my heart."

The lion bowed gravely to him and bounded away.

Ans followed the trail until it brought him at last to the forest at the edge of the sea. There it stopped, not far from a great heap of wood ash and blackened timbers. He saw that the party had taken ship across the sea. He looked right. He looked left. There was no ship or boat, no man in sight, and his heart sank.

Suddenly he heard a faint voice in the distance, and when he went toward it he found a cave from which came the voice of a man praying to Allah. Inside he found a hermit, who greeted him warmly, for Ans looked just like a fakir. His hair and beard had grown long and tangled. His face was haggard and weather-tanned. His one robe was torn and soiled from much traveling. No one would have guessed that only a few months before he was a handsome young captain in the Sultan's guard, dressed in rich silks with a scimitar at his side.

The hermit gave him fresh water, and berries to eat. Then Ans told his story, and the hermit said, "I lived here for twenty years without seeing man or woman. The wild beasts and the birds have been my only companions. But a few weeks ago I heard a great noise on the shore and saw a large party of men and women, camels and horses. There were carpenters who built a ship. They all sailed away in her, but five days later the ship returned with only a few men and camels. The men burned the ship on the shore and rode away."

"What can I do?" cried Ans, in despair. "I cannot build a ship. But I must follow my lady."

The hermit thought for a while. Then he said, "Go down to the palm grove by the seashore and bring me all the palm fiber that you can carry. I have a plan."

When Ans returned with the fiber the hermit twisted it into ropes and then made a net. "In the forest," he said, "you will find many hollow gourds, like great melons, and those that are dead and dried by the sun will float. If you will fill this net with them and tie it securely it will make a raft on which you can sail across the sea. And may Allah be with you."

Ans thanked the hermit and embraced him. Then he made his raft, carried it into the sea, and climbed onto it. There was a strong wind blowing from the land. Ans spread his robe like a sail, and the raft drove out across the sea, one wave lifting him up and the next bearing him down, soaking him with spray.

For three days and nights he sailed, always in danger, without food or water, and when the raft grounded at last on the beach below the Mountain of the Mother he was at his last gasp. But he soon found a stream of pure water, nuts and berries, and shellfish on the shore.

After a short rest he began to climb the mountain, and when he reached the top and saw the beautiful castle his heart leaped. "Surely," he said to himself, "Rose-in-bud must be there!"

The gate was bolted, so he sat down outside it. Soon the gatekeeper came out and said to him, "O holy man, where did you come from, and how did you come here?"

"I am a fakir of Ispahan," answered Ans. "I was voyaging across the sea and I was cast ashore on this island. I have traveled far."

The gatekeeper embraced him joyfully. "I too come from the fair city of Ispahan," he cried. "I never expected to see anyone from that city in this lonely place. The blessings of Allah on you! Come in, and rest and eat."

Ans found himself in a beautiful courtyard, surrounded by pillars of the finest marble. In the middle was a wide pool of water, shaded by flowering trees on which hung silver cages full of singing birds.

"What place is this?" he asked the gatekeeper. "Who built it?"

"Men built it long ago, and then left it empty," was the answer. "We do not know who or why. We are here because a certain Wazir has sent his daughter here, and sent us to serve and guard her, and keep her safe from all men."

Then Ans knew that Rose-in-bud was there. He ate gratefully the food which the gatekeeper set before him, the stewed goat's meat, the dates and oranges; he drank a long drink of cool sherbet, and he sat down to think how he might manage to see Rose-in-bud.

But he was too late. She had pined for Ans so long that she could bear it no longer; she made up her mind to go out into the world to look for him. Even while he was sitting in the courtyard, thinking about her, she was putting on her most beautiful dress, with earrings of rubies, a splendid necklace of diamonds and emeralds, and golden bracelets set with many jewels. She took all her other silk dresses in her arms and went up to her own private room. She knotted the dresses together to make a long, strong rope; she tied it to one of the big pillars and then she climbed down it to the rocks below. No one saw her. She walked along the seashore, wondering how she could escape, when Allah sent a fisherman to fish from his boat near the shore.

She called to him, and when he saw how beautiful she was, how richly dressed, he said to himself, "This is a princess, a great lady; she must be obeyed." So he took her into his boat, and at once a strong wind arose which blew them far across the Sea of Treasures, until they drew near a great city on the far side. The fisherman had never seen it before.

Now the King of this city was so brave and strong that he was known as Dirbas the Lion. He was looking out to sea when the fishing boat drove in to the land, and he was so surprised to see such a beautiful girl, so richly dressed, in such a boat, that he went down to the shore himself.

When they had greeted each other in the name of Allah he said, "Who are you, fair lady?"

"I am the daughter of Ibrahim, Grand Wazir to the Sultan Shamikh, O King. They call me Rose-in-bud." Then she told him her story.

The King was so sorry for her that he said, "You need have no more fear. If Allah wills, your trouble shall now be ended. I will adopt you as my daughter, and do all I can for you."

She gave the fisherman a jewel from one of her bracelets, which filled him with joy, and then she accompanied King Dirbas to his palace, where his maidens tended and bathed her and gave her food from the royal table.

The King commanded his Wazir to load a dozen camels with some of the finest treasures from the palace treasury, and to take them to the Sultan Shamikh, saying to him, "King Dirbas asks you to send to him at once the man named Ans al-Wujud, so that he can marry this young man to the most beautiful of his daughters."

The King knew that the Sultan would be afraid to refuse him, for he was a mighty King. So he said to his Wazir, "See to it that you bring back Ans al-Wujud with you. If you fail, I will disgrace you. I will make another Wazir in your place and forbid you ever to enter my palace again."

"I hear and I obey," replied the Wazir. He kissed the King's hands and set out at once on his journey to the Sultan Shamikh's court.

The Sultan heard him with dismay. "How gladly I would see Ans al-Wujud married to your King's daughter," he said, "but I cannot send him with you. He left us many months ago and no one knows where he has gone."

"I dare not go back without him," said the Wazir. "I must search until I find him."

"Then my Wazir Ibrahim shall go with you; he knows Ans," said the Sultan, and they set out the very next day. They searched east and they searched west, in city and village, forest and desert, asking everywhere for news of Ans and finding none. At long last they came to the castle on the Mountain of the Mother.

"This is the castle in which my daughter lives," said Ibrahim to the King's Wazir. "I shut her up here for fear that she and Ans al-Wujud would elope together. How glad I shall be to see her again!" He knocked at the great gate.

The gatekeeper knew the Wazir Ibrahim and kissed his hands and admitted them all. The first person they saw inside was Ans, who sat silent and miserable in the courtyard, for he had been told that Rose-in-bud had gone, no one knew where.

"Who is that strange man?" Ibrahim asked the gatekeeper.

"A fakir, a holy man of Ispahan, who sits lost in thought because he is so holy," answered the man.

Ibrahim passed by Ans and went into the castle, asking for Rose-in-bud, and the frightened servants told him that she had vanished. He searched the castle himself and found no trace of her. Then he asked for news of Ans, and no one had heard of him.

He went back to the King's Wazir. "Ans has not been here," he said, "and my daughter has vanished. I must go home at once to see whether she has returned. I must leave you to go on alone."

"Then I must go back to King Dirbas," he said, "and I will take this holy man with me. My only hope is that he may persuade the King to forgive me, or I am lost."

Ans agreed to go, not caring where he went now that he had lost Rose-in-bud. The two parties took ship together across the Sea of Treasures, and then the Wazirs went their different ways.

As the Grand Wazir drew near his city he became more and more afraid of what King Dirbas would do to him. Of course he did not know that the fakir was the very man he had been ordered to find, Ans al-Wujud, or that the strange lady whom he had seen at the King's court was Rose-in-bud. So he told the fakir his story, begging the fakir to plead for him with the angry King.

Ans was sorry for him, and said, "Fear nothing. Take me with you to the King and I promise you that I will cause Ans al-Wujud to appear."

"Is this true?" cried the Grand Wazir joyfully. "Can you really do this?"

"I swear it in the name of Allah," answered Ans.

Together they went to King Dirbas, who glared at the Grand Wazir and said, "Where is Ans al-Wujud?"

"He is very near," said the fakir. "I beg you, O King, to tell me why you want to see him, and I will bring him to your presence."

"It is a private matter," replied the King, and taking him into his own chamber he told him the whole story. You may be sure that Ans was almost overcome with joy, but he managed to say, "If your Majesty will leave me alone here, and will send me a handsome robe and your own barber, I can promise that you shall see Ans al-Wujud within the hour."

The King agreed readily. The barber came and trimmed the fakir's long beard and cut his hair short. The fakir washed thoroughly: he took off the dirty, ragged dress and put on the robe of blue silk embroidered with silver which the King had sent him. He was Captain Ans al-Wujud once again, and when he went back the King rose and embraced him. Then he sent for Rose-in-bud, who looked with wild eyes at the young man.

"It cannot be, it cannot be!" she whispered. She went pale as death, swayed and would have fallen, but Ans caught her in his arms.

What rejoicing there was then! Grand preparations were made at once. The Sultan Shamikh and Rose-in-bud's father and mother came to the wedding. For seven days and nights there was such feasting, minstrelsy, and merriment as the kingdom had never seen before, and the happiness of the young lovers was complete.

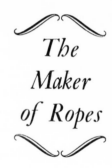

The
Maker
of Ropes

IN THE wonderful city of Baghdad, the city of peace, there lived two friends named Saadi and Saad. Saadi was very rich, and he always said that no one could be really happy unless he was rich, but his friend Saad laughed at this, saying, "I am not rich, but no one in Baghdad is happier than I am!"

One day when they were walking down the long line of shops in the bazaar together they had a great argument. Saadi said, "Anyone can make himself rich by working hard, if he has enough money to give him a start, but he must have this start, and he must work."

"That is the best way, and the surest way," said Saad, "but it is not the only way. Some men get rich by chance."

They went on arguing, until Saadi said, "Let us put it to the test."

They stopped outside a very small shop in which a rope-maker, who looked very poor, was hard at work.

"What is your name, my friend?" asked Saadi.

"My lord," replied the man, "my name is Hassan," and he bowed politely to his important-looking visitors.

"And you make ropes, I see. Are they good ropes?"

"Indeed they are," replied Hassan quickly. "There are none better in Baghdad. Fishermen and captains of ships come to my shop to buy them."

"Then why are you so poor?"

"I have no money, my lord," said Hassan very sadly. "By working hard all day long I earn only just enough to buy rice for my wife and my four children, charcoal for the stove, and oil for the lamp. I can never save enough to buy a large amount of hemp, and without that I cannot make my business grow."

"This is just the man we want," said Saadi to Saad; then he took a purse from his waistband and gave it to Hassan, saying, "Here are two hundred gold dinars. I give them to you in the name of Allah, and I hope your business will now prosper."

Hassan was so overcome that he could not speak. He fell on his knees and kissed the hem of Saadi's long silk robe. Then the two friends said goodbye to him and left him clutching his riches.

His first thought was, "Where can I put all this money to keep it safe?" There was no safe place for it in his little shop. At last he put ten gold dinars in his pocket, and took off his turban and tucked the purse into the long folds of cloth.

Then he went out. With six dinars he bought a small supply of hemp. Then he bought grapes, oranges, and a large piece of beef, for his family had had nothing but rice to eat

for many a day. Then a terrible thing happened. As he was walking along the street a starving vulture swooped down from the sky and tried to snatch the meat from him. He struggled so hard that his turban fell off and at once the vulture pounced on it and carried it away.

He screamed at the bird, and everyone in the street joined in, but it took no notice. Bird and turban were soon out of sight in the sky.

Poor Hassan! He had to buy a new turban, which left him

with very little money, and then he went home sadly to his wife Ayesha to tell her the story. She wept and wept, but he took it more quietly. "It is the will of Allah," he said very sadly. "I must not grumble. I must get on with my work."

A few months later Saad and Saadi paid Hassan another visit and were surprised to find him working as before. He told them what had happened.

"What!" cried Saadi angrily. "Do you expect us to believe that? Who ever heard of a vulture carrying off a turban? What have you done with the money?"

"By Allah, it is true, my lord," said Hassan miserably. "You can ask along the street. Many people saw it happen."

"There are many strange stories of vultures," said Saad, and Saadi soon forgot his anger, for he was a kindly man.

Taking out his purse he counted two hundred gold dinars onto Hassan's bench. "There," he said. "Let us try again and hope for better fortune." He would not wait for Hassan's thanks. Taking Saad's arm he went quickly away.

Hassan stared at the gold, hardly able to believe his eyes. "How can I keep it safe?" he asked himself. "I will take it home and find a safe hiding place."

So he tied the coins in a large piece of rag and with great care carried them home. Ayesha and all the children were out. He looked around anxiously. There were no cupboards; only a table and stools and cooking pots, and straw beds on the floor. The only possible place was an old pot full of bran which had stood untouched in a dark corner for months. He buried the gold deep in the bran and went back to his work.

Soon after his family came home a peddler went from

house to house selling washing balls, and Ayesha wanted to buy some, but she had no money at all. She looked wildly around the house for something which could be spared. Then she said to the peddler, "How many washing balls would you give me for this pot of bran?"

"Four," he answered.

"Oh," she said, "it is very good bran and a very good, strong pot. Could you not give me six?"

"Five," he answered.

He carried away the pot, while Ayesha set to work to boil rice on the charcoal stove for the family supper.

Very soon Hassan came home, and went straight to the dark corner where the pot had stood. It was gone!

"Ayesha," he cried in horror, "where is the pot of bran?"

"Oh, that old thing!" she answered. "I gave it to a peddler for five washing balls which I wanted badly."

"Who is he?" demanded her husband. "Where does he live? How can I find him?"

"I don't know," she answered, stirring the rice. "I've never seen him before."

Hassan tore his hair and his beard, and beat his breast. Then he told his wife about the two hundred gold dinars, and she burst into a flood of tears. "You should have told me," she wailed. "You should have told me they were there!" and all the children burst out crying in sympathy.

"They are gone," moaned Hassan. "There is no hope. It is the will of Allah that we should be poor." And next morning he went off miserably to his work.

Six months later Saad and Saadi once again passed that way,

and stopped at the shop to greet Hassan. He was so frightened
that he pretended not to see them until Saadi spoke to him.

"Well," asked Saadi, "how is it with you, Hassan? Have
you begun to grow rich?"

Hassan fell on his knees and tearfully told them about the
pot of bran.

"Stand up, man!" cried Saadi furiously. "How dare you
tell me such lies? What have you done with the money?"

"In the name of Allah, it is true!" wailed Hassan, beating
his breast.

"I believe you," said Saad. "Many stranger accidents have
happened."

He set to work to calm his friend, and presently Saadi said,
"Well, I have done. Now, Saad, perhaps you can show me
how this miserable man can get rich by accident. Money
doesn't help him."

Saad took out of his pocket a piece of lead, and gave it to
Hassan, saying, "I found this in the street just now. How
much is it worth?"

"Nothing," replied Hassan.

"Then keep it carefully until you have a use for it. Perhaps
it will bring you good fortune."

Obediently Hassan put it into his pocket and the two
friends went away.

Late that night there came a loud knocking at Hassan's
door, and when Ayesha opened it there was the wife of a
fisherman whom they knew. "My husband has lost the piece
of lead which weights his net," she said, "and if he can't go
fishing tonight we shall have nothing to eat tomorrow. The

shops are all shut, and I have asked all our other neighbors in vain. You are our last hope. Can you lend us a piece of lead?"

"Very gladly," answered Hassan, and groped about in the dark until he found it and gave it to her.

"Thank you a thousand times," she cried. "My husband will give you for this all the fish he catches in the first cast of his net tonight." And she went away happy.

Next morning she came back, carrying a very fine large fish. "This was the only one he caught in his first cast," she

said, "but it is the largest he has ever caught. It is yours for your kindness."

Thanking her warmly, Ayesha took the fish and cut it up for cooking. Inside it she found what she thought was a large smooth piece of glass, so she gave this to her children to play with and went on with her work.

The children, who had no toys, played with the piece of glass all day, and after dark they found that it gave out a beautiful light. They fell to quarreling over it, and made such a noise that Hassan stopped them to find out what it was all about. He told his wife to put out the oil lamp, and the glass shone so brightly that it lit the hut.

"See how lucky we are!" cried Hassan. "This piece of glass which we got for my piece of lead will save us from having to buy oil for the lamp in future."

The children were so excited by it that they made a great noise, until at last their father sent them to bed.

Now in the hut next door there lived a jeweler, who was too miserly to live in a good house although he was rich. Next morning his wife Rachel came to complain of the great noise which the children had made the previous night.

"I am very sorry," said Ayesha. "It won't happen again, and I hope you will forgive us. They got so excited over this piece of glass which I found in a fish. It's pretty, isn't it?"

"Yes, it is," said Rachel. "And do you know I've got a piece very like it. They would make a nice pair. Would you like to sell it to me?"

But the children who had heard all this, did not want to lose their toy, and began to cry, begging their mother not to sell it. So to quiet them she said, "No, thank you, Rachel," and the jeweler's wife went away.

She went straight to her husband's shop in the bazaar, to tell him about the piece of glass. Then she went back to Ayesha and beckoned her out of the hut so that they could talk without the children hearing.

"Ayesha," said she, "will you sell me that piece of glass for twenty gold dinars?"

At that moment Hassan came up, for it was dinnertime, so Ayesha asked whether he would accept Rachel's offer.

Hassan was silent, turning over in his mind what Saad had said about the piece of lead bringing him good fortune. Seeing him look so doubtful Rachel said to him quickly, too quickly, "Would you take fifty dinars?"

"No," he replied, for he was growing very suspicious. "I want a great deal more than that."

"A hundred dinars," said Rachel.

Now he felt sure. "No," he said. "For such a fine diamond as this I want a hundred thousand dinars. Nothing else."

"Oh, that's an impossible price," she cried. "No stone could be worth it. Come, neighbor, take twenty thousand while you can. You will be a rich man."

"A hundred thousand is my price," said he, "and that is because you are a neighbor. If I take it to a jeweler in the bazaar I shall ask more—and get it."

"Fifty thousand dinars," she said.

"No," he answered.

She sighed. "I cannot offer you more," she said. "I must ask my husband." And away she went.

It was not long before the jeweler himself appeared. "Good neighbor," he said, "will you show me this diamond of yours?"

He examined it lovingly, and at last he said, "My wife offered you fifty thousand gold dinars. I will give you twenty thousand more."

"No," said Hassan. "My price is one hundred thousand."

The jeweler haggled and argued, but it was no good; Hassan would not budge. Finally the jeweler agreed, and that night he gave Hassan ten leather bags, each containing ten thousand gold dinars.

Ayesha fell into Hassan's arms, weeping for joy, and the children all laughed and cried too, although they only half understood. "Let us give thanks to Allah," said Hassan. "I was wrong. He does not want us to remain poor."

Hassan would have gone to prostrate himself at the feet of Saad and Saadi, to thank them, but he had no idea where they lived. He gave a large gift of gold dinars to the fisherman and then set to work to build up his business. He went to see all the best ropemakers in Baghdad and arranged to buy from them at a fair price all the rope they could make; he promised to pay them promptly, which pleased them very much. He built a large warehouse to store the rope, with a shop where his clerks could sell it, and fine rooms for his family to live in. Very soon he was well known in Baghdad for his honesty and his riches. Now he and his wife and children had fine clothes and enough to eat.

Some time after this Saad and Saadi called at his little shop in the bazaar to see how he was getting on. They found the

shop empty but they were told where to find him and set
out at once for his new home and warehouse.

Hassan saw them coming. He ran to meet them and would
have stooped to kiss the hem of their robes. They would not
let him, and both embraced him. After he had thanked them
most warmly he led them into his fine house and seated them
in the place of honor. He sent for sweetmeats, and sherbet
and drinks scented with rose water, to refresh them, and then
told them his story.

"This is a fine tale," said Saadi, "but I believe it no more
than your tales of the vulture flying off with your turban or
your wife's giving away the pot of bran. I am sure that it was
the four hundred dinars I gave you which have made you
rich. But never mind. All that matters is that you have suc-
ceeded, and I am very glad."

"Nonsense!" cried Saad, with a laugh. "I am sure that all
three stories are true, and that it was my piece of lead which
brought him good fortune."

"My lords," said Hassan, "it is now growing late. If you
would honor my poor house by staying the night I should
like to take you tomorrow on a day's outing to the house in
the country which I have bought."

They both accepted gladly, and Hassan gave them a splendid feast, with music and singing, and dancers to entertain
them, for he was most anxious to show his gratitude to them
both.

Next morning early, while the air was still cool, they went
down to the great river Tigris, which flows through Baghdad. There a pleasure boat awaited them, with a rich awning

of green silk, comfortable divans, and fine Persian carpets under their feet. Thanks to six strong rowers they reached Hassan's country house beside the river in an hour and a half.

When he had shown them the house Hassan led them into the grove of orange and lemon trees in his beautiful garden, where the trees were laden with fruit and flowers, and a score of little streams ran musically, and the cool air was full of the scent of flowers and the song of many birds.

The garden ended in a grove of tall trees, where the air was cooler still. They found Hassan's two little boys playing there, with a servant to look after them. They had just seen a very large nest in one of the tallest trees, so they asked the servant to climb up and get it for them.

When he came down with it he found to his astonishment that it was in a turban, and the little boys ran with it to their father.

Hassan knew it at once. Showing it to his two guests he said, "My lords, do you think this turban has been long in that tree?"

"It looks as though it has been there for many months," answered Saadi, "and the nest inside it is an old one."

"Let us sit down," said Hassan, and led them to a stone seat. There he took out the nest, while they watched, and unwound the cloth of the turban until there fell out of it, with a chinking of coins, the large purse which Saadi had given him on his first visit.

Hassan emptied the purse onto the bench and asked Saadi to count the coins. There were a hundred and ninety gold dinars.

"This," said Hassan, "is the turban which the vulture flew away with."

"There can be no doubt about it," said Saadi. "You have shown us, friend Hassan, that your first tale was true, and I believe now that the other tales were true also. I hope you will forgive me for having doubted you."

"That I will gladly," replied Hassan, "for I owe all my good fortune to you and Saad."

Saadi turned to Saad and said with a smile, "This has shown that I was wrong and you were right. A man may sometimes get rich by a fortunate chance."

The
Bird
Princess

MEN say that long ago, in the city of Basra, there lived a young goldsmith named Hassan. He had a shop in the bazaar, which was the street of shops, and there he worked at his trade. He had many tools, a charcoal fire, and a tube through which he blew the fire to make it burn fiercely. He was clever with his hands, and made many beautiful things of gold.

He was also a charming, good-looking young man. His father was dead and he lived alone with his mother, who looked after him very well.

One evening he was busy in his shop when a stranger came in. He was a tall, dignified man with a high white turban, a dark face, and a white beard. He wore a long dark robe and carried a book which looked very old. For a few minutes he watched Hassan at work on a fine gold chain. Then he saluted Hassan, who rose and bowed.

"Young man," said the stranger, "something draws me strongly to you. What is your name?"

"I am called Hassan."

"I am Bahram the Persian."

Hassan bowed again.

"Hassan," said the Persian, "I have no son, and the moment I saw you something seemed to tell me that I could love you as my son. Will you let me adopt you and teach you my art?"

"My lord," answered Hassan, "you do me too much honor. What is your art?"

"It is a secret art," replied Bahram. "Hundreds of people have asked me to teach them, and I have refused them all. But I would teach you if you became my son, and I can tell you that it would make you rich for life."

The Persian was so grand and serious that Hassan could not help believing him. "Oh, sir," cried Hassan, "I could ask nothing better in this world. When will you begin to show me your art?"

"Tomorrow," answered Bahram. "You make me very happy. And now goodbye until the morning." He took Hassan's head between his hands, kissed him gently on the forehead, and went away.

Hassan was too excited to do any more work. He shut his shop and hurried home as fast as he could to tell his mother. But she was not at all pleased with his news. She cried out in horror, "A Persian! He cannot be a Moslem, a true believer. He does not worship Allah, as we do. He worships fire. He is a magician. There is no saying what evil he will do you."

"Mother," answered Hassan, "he wears a white turban,

like a Moslem. He is a good and noble man, I feel sure. He will bring us nothing but riches and happiness."

All she could say was useless. Hassan would not listen. Next morning he hurried to his shop as soon as daylight came. It was not long before the Persian came in, and they greeted each other affectionately. Then Bahram asked, "Have you a brass dish in this shop?"

Hassan brought a large one at once, and Bahram said, "Now break it into small pieces and throw them into the crucible in which you melt your gold. Then put it over your fire."

Hassan did as he was told, and blew up the charcoal fire with his blowpipe until the brass was melted and boiling hot.

Then Bahram read strange words from the ancient book which he carried, and passed his hands three times over the boiling, bubbling brass. He took a little package from the folds of his turban, and emptied a powder from it into the crucible. There was a blinding flash of light and instantly the melted brass turned into a solid bar of gold.

Too excited to speak, Hassan lifted the bar out with his tongs. It was quite cold!

"Now test it," said Bahram, and Hassan soon found that it was indeed the purest, finest gold. He took the magician's hands and kissed them reverently.

"Now," said Bahram, "take this gold to the market and sell it. But remember, you must not tell anyone where it came from. Say that you are selling it for a friend of yours."

You may be sure that Hassan lost no time. He sold the gold bar for fifteen thousand gold dinars. This was great riches to

him. Taking the money, he hurried home to his mother to
tell her all about it, thinking that this would make her happy.
But she burst into tears and sobbed, "This is alchemy, black
magic! It is forbidden. This man must be a servant of the Evil
One. Leave him, my son, leave him before it is too late!"

"No, no, Mother," cried Hassan. "I am sure he is a good
man. And we shall be rich."

He kissed her, and took a brass bowl which his mother
used for making salads, and hurried back to his shop.

"I sold the bar for fifteen thousand dinars," he said to Bahram. "Here they are."

"Five thousand of them are yours," answered the magician,
putting them into a purse and handing them back.

Hassan kissed his hands and thanked him again and again.
Then Bahram said, "What do you mean to do with that brass
bowl?"

"Make it into gold," said Hassan, putting more charcoal
on his fire. "Will you not teach me how to do it?"

"Do you really think I can teach you here in this shop,
when anybody might come in? We should be taken before
the judge, who would have us put to death. But if you will
take me to your house, and bring all your tools, we can work
in secret."

So Hassan led the way to his house, and left Bahram at the
corner of the street until he had persuaded his mother to go
and see one of her friends. Then he seated the Persian in the
best room while he went to the market and brought back
dishes of the finest roast chicken, and rice, and a loaf of white
bread, saucers of jellies, jams, and sweetmeats of all kinds,
and a flask of red wine.

"Let us eat, my lord," he said, "and when we have eaten bread and salt together we shall be bound never to harm each other. May Allah take revenge on any traitor to bread and salt!"

"So be it," answered Bahram, smiling. "Let us eat."

When they had finished he said, "Now, my son, let us set to work."

Hassan broke up the brass bowl, threw the pieces into his crucible, and put it on his mother's charcoal fire. Then he blew on the fire until the brass had melted, when Bahram did his magic as before. Hassan lifted the bar, and laid it on his scales.

Unseen by Hassan, Bahram took a very strong drug from a pocket and pushed it into one of the sweetmeats.

"My son," he said, "this sweetmeat is so delicious, you must try it."

Hassan put it into his mouth, and fell down as if he were dead.

"Now you are mine!" cried Bahram. He tied up Hassan's legs and arms with silk scarves, he emptied all the clothes from a large wooden chest, crammed Hassan into it, and locked it fast. He emptied another chest and put into it the bar of gold and everything valuable which he could find in the house. Then he fetched porters from the marketplace to carry the two chests.

He led them to the riverside, where a ship was waiting, and as soon as the chests had been carried down to Bahram's cabin the captain sang out to the sailors to weigh anchor and set sail.

They sailed down the river Tigris and far, far across the

sea to a lonely island in which a great mountain rose almost into the clouds. Bahram had the two chests carried to the beach, which was covered with pebbles of many colors, red, white, yellow, and sky-blue. There he stood watching the ship until it was out of sight.

Then he took Hassan out of the chest and flung him down on the pebbles, and hid both chests among some bushes nearby. Next he untied Hassan's hands and feet, and blew a green powder into his nostrils.

Hassan sneezed three times. Rubbing his eyes he sat up and looked to the right and looked to the left. You can guess how surprised he was. Then he was very frightened.

"Where are we?" he cried. "Why have you brought me here?"

"We are on a secret island, far from your city," answered the magician. "I have brought you here to sacrifice you to the god of fire, whom I worship. Every year I bring a Moslem youth here and kill him on the top of this mountain."

"Traitor!" cried Hassan. "You have broken the bond of bread and salt. Allah will punish you!" He staggered to his feet. Bahram laughed and knocked him down. Again he got to his feet, and again Bahram gave him a great blow which knocked him down. He lay groaning, for the magician had the strength of three men.

Bahram took from his robe a little drum made of copper, with a silk strap, and he beat on the drum. The sun was blotted out by a black cloud, and at the seventh stroke there came flying out of the cloud a great scarlet eagle. It came to earth, and the cloud vanished.

Bahram flung Hassan across the giant bird's neck and leaped onto its back. They rose in the air, the eagle's wings beating with a sound like the wings of a hundred swans. Higher and higher they flew, until the bird came down on the flat top of the mountain. Bahram threw Hassan to the ground, and dismounted. The eagle vanished into air.

The magician set Hassan on his feet and said, "Now watch, and again you shall see my power. I will summon fire."

He stepped back and took the little drum from his robe. He did not see that he was standing on the edge of a precipice. But Hassan saw it. He leaped forward and thrust him backward over the cliff. The magician dropped the drum, he clutched wildly at the air, and then with a terrible cry he fell, to be dashed to pieces on the rocks far below.

Hassan was free! He put the little drum into the pocket of his robe. He looked about him, he looked right and he looked left, and there not far away was a splendid palace, flashing in the sunshine. He hurried toward it.

The main gate of the palace stood open between pillars of shining gold, so he walked boldly into the courtyard. It was shaded by flowering trees and cooled by splashing fountains. There were bright beds of flowers which filled the air with their sweet scents.

Two young princesses were sitting on a marble bench, playing chess. Hassan looked at them with admiration, for they were both more beautiful than any human girl could be, and both beautifully dressed in fine silks. They looked at Hassan in great surprise, and the younger said, "Fair sir, how did you come here?"

Hassan bowed low and answered. "I was brought to the mountaintop by Bahram the magician."

"That evil man!" she cried. "He must have brought you to the mountain to kill you. How did you escape?"

"I killed him," said Hassan. "I thrust him over the cliff and he died on the rocks below."

"Allah be praised!" cried the other princess. "We thank you with all our hearts. You have rid us of a terrible enemy. Hairs would grow on my tongue before I could tell you all the evils he has done."

"What is your name?" said the younger.

"I am called Hassan, and I am of Basra," he answered. He smiled at her.

"My name is Peach-blossom," she said, smiling. She and Hassan took a great liking to each other at once. She turned to her sister and said, "I ask you to bear witness that I take this young man for my brother, and I will care for him as a sister should care for her brother."

"I bear witness gladly, O my sister," said the other.

"And I take you as my sister," said Hassan to Peach-blossom. He kissed her on the forehead and she returned the kiss.

"My name is Almond-flower," said the older girl. "There are seven of us here, all sisters. Our five elder sisters are all out riding. Our father is one of the great kings of the Jinn, the spirits of air. He has made up his mind to keep us from getting married, and he has put us on this mountaintop so that no man can come near us. I do not understand how you got here. It must be the will of Allah."

"We are guarded and waited on by slaves of the Jinn whom you cannot see," said Peach-blossom.

She spoke strange words into the air, and golden goblets were handed to them by invisible hands. Hassan found that his contained ice-cold sherbet water and he drank it gratefully.

"You must be tired and hungry," said Peach-blossom. "Come with me."

Taking his hand, she showed him the chamber which was to be his, and the bathhouse, and while he bathed a feast was laid under the trees in the courtyard. Then the other five sisters came home. They were all very glad to see Hassan, and soon the eight of them were eating, drinking, and talking together, waited on by invisible hands.

Their life went on happily for weeks. The sun always shone on them. The palace was very large and wonderful. The floors, pillars, and walls were of many-colored marble, adorned with paintings. The floors were covered with rich carpets and tapestries. There were divans and cushions everywhere, and fountains and rivulets of running water. Sweetly scented airs floated through the rooms, and soft music played by invisible musicians. Peach-blossom showed Hassan everything. But she never took him to the roof, and when he wanted to go up the staircase which led to it she clutched his arm and cried, "No, no, it is forbidden!" Three times this happened. Then he did not try again.

One morning they heard a noise far away. They looked out of the palace gate and saw a large cloud of dust coming nearer.

"That must be a company of horsemen, messengers from our father," said Peach-blossom to Hassan. "No one else ever comes. Quick! You must hide. If they find you here they will kill you. Go into your chamber and lock the door, and stay there until I come for you."

"I hear and I obey," replied Hassan, laughing. He heard the clatter of hoofs in the courtyard and men's voices. Then there came a very soft knock on his door and when he opened it Peach-blossom slipped in quietly.

"The messengers are taking us all back to our father at once," she whispered. "He is giving a great feast and wants us to be there. We shall be back in a week's time. I have commanded the slaves to look after you and obey you. And remember, it is forbidden to go on the roof. Goodbye, dear brother." She kissed him and hurried away.

When they had all gone Hassan wandered about the palace, feeling more and more lonely, until at last he said to himself. "I know what I can do. Now is my chance to go on the roof."

Very quietly he went up the long, curving staircase, looking for danger and seeing none. Then he found himself in the most wonderful garden he had ever seen. It covered the whole roof of the great palace and in the middle of it was a wide pool of sparkling water. There were flowering trees and bushes all round the pool, and it seemed that on every branch a bird was singing.

Hassan was enchanted. He wandered about the garden until the sun had set and the moon had risen, a full moon in a cloudless sky. At last he began to feel hungry, and turned to go down into the palace. Suddenly he heard a sound of wings, and looking up he saw ten large white birds flying toward the garden. He hid behind a tree to watch them. They swooped down and landed beside the pool. They shed their feathered skins and out of them came ten maidens. All were beautiful, but one of them shone like the full moon. She was far lovelier than any human girl could be, and she made Hassan's heart stand still. From that moment he was madly in love with her. He could not take his eyes off her. Soon he saw that she was the leader, and he thought that she must be a great princess and that the other girls were her attendants.

They danced along the edge of the pool. Then they all dived in and swam to and fro, splashing, laughing, and playing tricks on each other. But none of them played tricks on the princess. They went on enjoying themselves, and Hassan watched, until the moon began to set. Then they sprang out out of the pool, slipped into their bird dresses, and flew away.

Hassan watched them until they were out of sight. Then he went sadly down into the palace. He had fallen in love with a fairy princess. What was he to do? He could not sleep or eat, he could think of nothing but that wonderful girl, but although he watched every night she did not come again. Now he knew why Peach-blossom had kept him from going onto the roof.

When the seven sisters came back they found Hassan looking so thin and so ill that they all cried out in alarm. Peach-blossom soon made him tell her what had happened, and the sisters turned pale and trembled.

"This is terrible," said Peach-blossom. "Your fairy princess is the Princess Splendor, one of the daughters of the supreme King of the Jinn. My father and all the other Kings obey him. The roof garden is hers. Only she and her hand-maidens are allowed to enter it. If the King her father heard that you had been there he would kill us all. He would never give her in marriage to anyone but a great King. You must forget her. It is the only way."

"Never!" cried Hassan. "If I cannot marry her I shall die." He flung himself on his bed and would not listen to any of the sisters.

A week went by. Hassan could not eat or sleep. Peach-blossom saw that he would indeed die, and at last she said, "There is one thing you could do. It is very dangerous but it is your only hope."

Hassan opened his eyes and looked at her. "The Princess will come again, as she always does, at the next full moon. I will tell you what you must do then, but if you fail it will be the death of all of us." She told him what to do, and then he let her persuade him to eat and drink.

When the night of the full moon came Hassan hid himself among the trees in the roof garden. Soon he heard the sound of wings. The ten beautiful white birds swooped down, slipped out of their bird dresses, and dived into the water as before. Hassan waited until they were all on the far side of the pool. Then he crept very quietly among the trees to the place where they had left their feathers. He snatched up the Princess's dress and hid it deep among the bushes.

When they were tired of swimming and playing they came back to dress. The Princess stood still in horror. "My dress!" she screamed. "My dress has gone!"

They gathered around her, all talking at once. They searched the garden far and wide, but Hassan had hidden himself and the dress so cleverly that they could not find them. Suddenly one girl called out, "The moon is setting!" Then with cries of fear they sprang into the air and flew away, leaving the Princess alone.

This was the moment for which Hassan had been waiting. He leaped from his hiding place and seized her by the hair. In vain she struggled and begged him to let her go. He marched her off to Peach-blossom's chamber and shut her in. Then he told Peach-blossom what he had done. "I will go to the Princess," she said.

The Princess cried and stormed and threatened until she was tired out. Then Peach-blossom told her what a kind and charming young man Hassan was, and how he had been dying for love of her. "He will never do you any harm," she said. "He wants to marry you, and you could not possibly have a better husband."

The Princess stormed and wept again, but in the end she dried her tears and agreed to see Hassan. He kissed her hands in homage, and begged her to forgive him. She liked him so much that she could not help smiling at him through her tears.

For seven days he wooed her gently, until she threw her arms around him and said she would marry him. So next day they were married by the rites of Allah, and the seven sisters gave them a splendid wedding feast under the trees in the courtyard.

For twenty-one weeks Hassan and Splendor lived very happily in the palace. Then Hassan had a dream which worried him. He dreamed that he went back to his mother's house in the city of Basra and found her very unhappy and very ill because she had had no news of him. She felt sure that the magician had carried him off and she thought he must be dead.

When he told his wife and the sisters about his dream they all said that he must go back to his mother at once. So he and Splendor got ready for the journey.

Peach-blossom knew that he was a poor man, and she gave him as a parting present two large leather bags full of precious jewels, enough to make him rich for life. She gave Splendor some of her own most beautiful dresses, and she told the invisible slaves to get together everything needed for the journey.

That evening the sisters gave them a farewell feast, and Peach-blossom made Hassan promise to come and see them as soon as he could. Next morning Hassan beat on the little drum which had belonged to the magician. In a moment the giant scarlet eagle came swooping down into the courtyard. He drummed again and the eagle vanished. He drummed twice and two great camels came trotting through the main gate into the palace courtyard, and knelt down to be loaded. They were the largest that Hassan had ever seen.

Then the unseen slaves loaded the bags of jewels, clothes, and food. Hassan and Splendor said goodbye to all the sisters and mounted the camels. "To Basra!" cried Hassan, and the two camels went like the wind over desert and river, sea and mountain. They went so fast that by evening they reached Hassan's house.

He tethered the camels at the door and went in, to find his mother sitting sadly alone. She threw herself into his arms and wept for joy. Then he led in Splendor, and the house was filled with light, as though the full moon had risen.

"O my lady," cried Hassan's mother, "I welcome you with all my heart, but this poor house of ours is no place for you."

"I have brought home great riches as well as a beautiful wife," said Hassan. "Tomorrow I will buy a palace."

"Not in Basra," said his mother. "Everyone here knows that we are poor. If we suddenly become rich they may pester and rob us. Let us go to Baghdad, the city of peace, where no one knows us. There we shall be safe under the great Caliph, the Commander of the Faithful, Haroun al-Rashid."

"How wise you are," said Hassan. "We will go tomorrow."

He brought his goods into the house, and struck twice on the little drum. The two camels vanished.

That night he told his mother all his adventures, and next morning they took ship on the river Tigris and went to Baghdad. There Hassan bought a fine palace and furnished it beautifully. There they all lived happily to the end of their days.

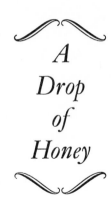

A
Drop
of
Honey

THERE was a hunter who used to hunt wild beasts among the mountains, and his dog, of which he was very fond, always went with him.

One day when it was raining hard he took shelter in a cave and there he found a wild bees' nest full of honey. The bees had all left it, so he emptied the water from his water-skin, and filled it with honey. Then he threw the skin over his shoulder and carried it to the city.

He went to the shop of a merchant who sold honey and oils, who tasted the honey and then said he would buy it all.

The huntsman emptied it out of the skin into a dish on the merchant's counter, and he spilled a drop of honey on the ground. At once the flies began to buzz around it, and then a bird swooped down from a neighboring tree and began to eat the flies.

The merchant's favorite cat, which was sitting on a bench, sprang upon the bird, and at that the huntsman's dog leaped on the cat and killed her.

The merchant was so enraged by this that he snatched up a knife and killed the dog. This was too much for the hunter. Drawing his long knife from his belt he stabbed the merchant to the heart. Then he fled for his life.

Now the merchant came from one village and the huntsman from another, and as soon as the people of the two places heard what had happened they took up their swords and spears and went out against each other.

When the two lines met there was terrible fighting between them until both sides were beaten. No one knows how many men lost their lives, how many wives lost their husbands, how many children lost their fathers.

For a drop of honey.

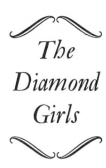

The Diamond Girls

WHEN the good Sultan of Basra died, his young son Zain became Sultan in his place. Zain was a silly boy. His only idea was to enjoy himself. He chose friends as foolish as himself to help him rule the country, and very soon they spent all the money in the royal treasury. No one looked after the country's affairs and they went from bad to worse.

At last the Queen, Zain's mother, went to him and said, "You are ruining your country, and the people are so angry that very soon they will rebel and kill you!"

This was a great shock to Zain. He saw that he must take his mother's advice. He sent away his bad companions, and chose as his new ministers the best men he could find. They began to put the country in order, to give justice in the courts of law and put down robbers everywhere.

But Zain and his mother were now very poor and this made him miserable because it was all his fault. Then one night he dreamed that a strange old man came to him and said, "Sultan, you must go to the great city of Cairo. You must go

alone, in disguise, and on foot. Then you will find a cure
for your misery."

The dream was so real that the very next day he set off,
disguised as a poor merchant. He left the Queen to rule the
country. It was a long journey and he had a very hard time;
he was hunted by wild beasts, and he had to fight with robbers. But he faced all dangers bravely, and one evening he
arrived safely at the great gate of Cairo. He was so tired that
he lay down on the ground outside a mosque. He fell fast
asleep at once, and he dreamed again of the old man, who
said to him, "I told you to take this journey only as a test.
You have shown yourself brave and strong, and you deserve
good fortune. Go back now to your palace in Basra. Take
a little pickax and dig in your father's private chamber.
There you will find riches and something which is more im-
portant, happiness."

Tired as he was, Zain set out next morning, and he took
little rest until he had reached his palace and greeted his
mother. But he did not tell her his dream. He bathed and
slept well. Next morning he told a servant to bring him a
pickax, and set to work to dig up the marble floor of his
father's private chamber.

It was heavy work. He dug for hours, finding nothing, but
he would not give in. Then at last he uncovered an iron ring
set in a stone slab. He pulled up the slab, and there was a
marble staircase winding down into the earth.

You may be sure it did not take him long to light a lamp
and hurry down that staircase. He found himself in a large
room, with a floor of china tiles, and walls and ceiling of

crystal in which the little flame of his lamp was reflected a thousand times. In the room were four large tables made of gold, and on each table stood ten large vases of polished red marble. Lifting the cover of one of them, he found that it was full of gold coins, hundreds of them. All the forty vases were the same.

Overjoyed, he ran quickly to the Queen, and brought her to see the treasure he had found.

"Now we shall never be poor again," she cried, "and you will be able to rule your kingdom well!"

She walked around the room. In one corner stood a little vase which Zain had not noticed. She lifted the cover and found a golden key inside.

"Look!" she cried. "This may lead us to more treasure."

Together they searched the walls of the room, foot by foot, until at last they found a small keyhole hidden in a rose carved in the crystal.

Zain turned the key in the lock, and they stepped into another crystal room, even more beautiful than the first. But here there were no marble vases. Ranged around the room were nine pedestals of gold, and on eight of them stood statues of lovely maidens, each statue carved from a single diamond. They filled the room with a splendor of light. Zain and the Queen stood in rapture, unable at first to move or speak.

Then Zain looked at the ninth pedestal, on which there was nothing except a piece of white satin, bearing words written in the finest Persian handwriting. He went to it and read aloud: " 'My son, it cost me much trouble and much money to obtain these eight statues, which I leave to you with my love. But beautiful and valuable as they are, there is a ninth in the world which is far finer. It is worth ten thousand such statues as these. I charge you to find it. In Cairo there lives a former slave of mine, named Mobrek. He is now a rich merchant. He is the only man who has helped me to find these statues. Go to him, and he will tell you how to find the ninth. Your father.' "

Zain and his mother looked at each other. "I must go again to Cairo," he said.

"Indeed you must, my son," she answered.

So next day the Sultan set out again for Cairo, but this time he was dressed in robes of silk. A dozen men of his body-guard went with him, well armed. They were all mounted on black horses.

When they reached Cairo they asked for Mobrek's house and were directed to it at once, for he was well known as one of the richest and kindest merchants in the city. His house was a palace.

"Who are you?" asked the porter at the great marble doorway. "What do you want?"

"I am a stranger from Basra," answered the Sultan, "and I ask for lodging in your master's house."

A slave went to tell Mobrek, and soon came back saying that he wished to see the stranger. Zain followed the slave into a great pillared hall, where Mobrek, rising from his chair, greeted Zain politely. He was a tall man, richly dressed, with a flowing gray beard.

"Who are you, honored sir?" he asked.

"I am Zain, son of your former master, the Sultan of Basra, who has gone to his peace."

Mobrek looked at him. "It is news to me that the Sultan had a son," he said. "How old are you?"

"I am twenty," replied Zain.

"Ah," said Mobrek, "it is twenty-two years since I left Basra. Can you show that you are the Sultan's son?"

Zain took from the folds of his turban the piece of white satin, and said, "I found this on the ninth pedestal in the secret chamber of the diamond girls."

Mobrek prostrated himself at Zain's feet.

"My lord," he said, "I was your father's slave. Therefore I am your slave, and everything which I have is yours."

Zain stooped and raised him to his feet.

"O my lord," Mobrek said, "what can I do for you?"

"Only show me how to find the ninth diamond girl," replied Zain.

"The search will be dangerous," said Mobrek. "But I can show you the way. We can start tomorrow. And I hope, my lord, that tonight you will honor my poor house with your presence."

Next day, after the morning prayers, Sultan Zain and Mobrek set out, with the Sultan's guard and Mobrek's servants behind them. They rode through the desert for seven days, sleeping every night under the stars. They saw no other living thing. At last Mobrek reined in his horse, saying, "My lord, you and I must now go on alone."

They dismounted, and Mobrek took two small rugs of a strange pattern from one of his servants. They walked quickly until they came to the shore of a great lake.

"Now, my lord," said Mobrek, "we are in the land of the Jinn, the spirits of fire and air. You know that they show themselves sometimes as beautiful human beings, sometimes as animals, sometimes as the most horrible monsters. You must be prepared to face them. Only the Prince of the Jinn can give you the precious maiden you seek, and we must cross this lake to find him."

"How can we cross it?" asked Zain. "We have no boat!"

As he spoke a boat suddenly appeared on the lake, a red boat flying a blue satin flag, which rowed swiftly toward them. The oarsman had the head of an elephant and the body of a tiger.

"Whatever may happen," said Mobrek, "you must not speak a single word while we are in this boat. If you do, it will sink at once and we shall both be drowned."

"I will be silent," replied Zain.

The boat came to shore. The oarsman picked them up, one after the after, with his elephant's trunk and put them into his boat. He rowed swiftly across the lake until he came to a large island, where he lifted them ashore. Next moment he and his boat had disappeared.

"Now we may talk," said Mobrek. "Have you ever seen a land as beautiful as this?"

"Never," answered Zain, looking about him. "It is a Paradise." Sweetly scented flowers of many colors bloomed at their feet as they walked, they were shaded from the sun by green and gracious trees, and all the birds in the world seemed

to be singing in the branches. Every step showed them new beauties.

At length they came to a splendid palace. The walls were of emerald. A wide moat surrounded it and along the bank grew tall trees which shaded the whole palace. The massive gates were of gold, and the bridge which led to them was made of the shell of a gigantic shellfish. The gate was guarded by Jinn warriors, very tall and fierce, whose spears glittered in the sun.

"If we go nearer," said Mobrek, "the Jinn will kill us."

He spread on the ground the two rugs he was carrying, and took from a pocket a bunch of herbs which he sprinkled along the borders of the rugs, muttering strange words as he did so. Then he motioned to Zain to sit on one of the rugs and seated himself on the other.

"My lord," he said, "I shall now conjure the Prince of the Jinn, who lives in this palace. If he is angry with us for coming he will appear as a dreadful monster. If he is willing to help us he will be a handsome man. Whatever his shape you must rise and bow low to him, and you must not step off your mat. If you do you will be lost. You must say to him, 'Lord of the Jinn, I beseech you to befriend me as you befriended my father, and I beg you, most humbly, to give me the ninth maiden.' "

Then Mobrek lifted his arms toward the palace and spoke strange and terrible words of power. There was a blinding flash of lightning, a peal of thunder which shook the earth under them, and darkness fell on the whole island. Then a great wind swept the darkness away, and in the sunshine there appeared a tall and terrible but handsome Prince.

He smiled on Zain. "I loved your father," he said, "and every time he came to pay his respects to me I gave him one of the diamond statues. Just before he died I asked him to write the message which you found, and I told him I would give you the ninth statue. I was the old man whom you saw in your dreams. But you must do as I tell you. You must find a very beautiful young maiden who is fifteen years old, but has never wished to be married. You must bring her to me and you must not try to keep her for yourself."

"How shall I know when I have found the right one?" asked Zain.

"I will give you a small mirror, in which you will see her face when you have found her. Until then it will be clouded over. Now you must swear that you will obey me."

Zain swore by the name of Allah that he would.

"I am pleased with you, my son," said the Prince of the Jinn. "Here is the mirror. Now go, and come back as soon as you can."

There was a terrible crash of thunder, and the Prince vanished.

Zain and Mobrek went back to the shore of the island. The elephant-headed Jinnee rowed them across as before, and very soon they were riding away with their followers.

When they reached Cairo again Mobrek said, "I know a clever old lady here who is a marriage broker and arranges most of our marriages."

She brought all the most beautiful fifteen-year-old maidens in the city for Zain to see, but it was no use. His mirror was still clouded over.

"The trouble is," said Mobrek, "that they all want to get married."

So they went to the great city of Baghdad, which was ruled over by the famous Haroun al-Rashid, the Commander of the Faithful, on whom be peace. There they found lodgings for themselves and stables for all their horses at an inn, a large caravanserai. Mobrek had a friend in Baghdad, an old man who was well known because he did so much to help the poor. Mobrek took him a purse containing five hundred gold pieces, to be given to sick people in need, as a present from the Sultan Zain.

Next day the old man came to see Zain and Mobrek, to thank them. They told him why they were in Baghdad, and he said at once that he knew of a maiden who might be the one they sought. She was the daughter of a Wazir, or minister, of the Caliph Haroun.

He took them to the Wazir, who welcomed them warmly when he heard that Zain was Sultan of Basra. He soon sent for his fifteen-year-old daughter whose name was Aisha. When she came he told her to take off her veil.

Zain drew a deep breath. She was the most beautiful girl he had ever seen. He looked in his magic mirror and saw her face in it. This was the maiden whom he sought! He asked the Wazir's permission to marry her, a lawyer was sent for, and arrangements for the marriage were made. Zain gave the Wazir a rich present of gold and jewels, and next day the wedding feast was held, with great rejoicing.

"She is so charming," said Zain to Mobrek, "that I wish I could carry her to Basra and make her my queen."

"May Allah forbid!" cried Mobrek. "If you do, the Prince of the Jinn will strike you both dead!"

So when Zain's party rode away, with Aisha in a litter carried by two horses, they did not take the way of the caravans to Basra. They rode into the desert.

Zain had not seen or spoken to Aisha since the wedding; he was afraid that he would want to keep her instead of giving her to the Jinn. But on the third day she said to Mobrek, "O friend of my lord, how long is it before we come to my lord's city of Basra?"

"Alas, my lady," answered Mobrek. "The time has come to tell you the cruel truth. My lord did not promise to take you to Basra or to make you his queen. He married you only to give you to the Prince of the Jinn, who commanded him to bring such a maiden as you are."

Aisha burst into tears and wept bitterly. It made Zain's heart ache to hear her, but he was afraid to try to comfort her. There was nothing for it but to ride on, and when they reached the island he gave her to the Prince.

"You have done well," said the Prince. "You have obeyed me at every point. Now go back to your palace, and on the ninth pedestal you will find the most wonderful statue of all, worth ten thousand times as much as all the others."

So they rode for Basra, and Zain's heart was heavy. He knew that it would have been certain death for Aisha and for himself if he had disobeyed the Prince of the Jinn. But he knew that he had treated her cruelly, and lost her forever. He loved her now with his whole heart.

When they reached the palace at last, he went sadly to his father's chamber and unlocked the door. He pulled up the flagstone and went slowly down the marble staircase into the room of treasures. He took the little golden key from its place and opened the secret door.

On the ninth pedestal, clad in a long white robe covered with glittering diamonds, stood Aisha!

With a great cry of joy Zain took her into his arms.

One
Winter
Night

THE famous Caliph of Baghdad, Haroun al-Rashid, had a master musician, a very sweet singer, whose name was Ishak. It was to Ishak that this wonder happened.

One cold winter night the streets were full of driving rain, as though the black clouds were emptying their waterskins on the earth. On this night Ishak sat alone in his little house, crouching over the charcoal brazier to keep himself warm, for the bitter wind seemed to blow through doors and shutters, although they were firmly closed. As he listened to the wind and rain, his heart grew heavier. In such weather no one would visit him, and he could not go out through the rain and the deep mud to visit his friends. He must spend the evening alone, a thing he rarely did.

His servant laid supper on the table, but he was too miserable to eat, and as he sat there he began to dream of his sweetheart, the beautiful Zayda, who was a slave girl in the Caliph's palace. The more he thought of her the more he longed to see her, and suddenly he cried aloud, "I wish Zayda were here!" He was startled by his voice, for he had called very loudly. He was still more startled a moment later, when there came a knocking at his door.

"Someone who has lost his way in the storm," he thought. He went quickly and opened the door, and there stood Zayda!

Her green silk dress and the veil of gold brocade which covered her head were soaked, she was splashed from head to foot with mud, and mud caked her little shoes. Ishak drew her into the room, shut and bolted the door, and led her to the brazier. Her coming seemed to fill the room with the perfume of flowers.

"Dear girl," cried Ishak, "how could you come out in such a night as this?"

"How could I not come?" she answered. "Your messenger said you were alone and miserable, and longing to see me. How could I not come to you?"

For a moment Ishak's heart stood still with fear. He had sent no messenger. But he would not frighten her with this. He drew her to him and kissed her. She was trembling with cold. Then he brought her a fine towel and a silk robe of his own to put on. He called his servant to bring a bowl of warm water from the kitchen, and he washed her feet, and poured essence of roses over them. He made up the brazier and trimmed the candles. Very soon they were both warm and happy.

"Will you share my supper?" said Ishak. "There is roast chicken, figs, and oranges."

"No thank you, my love," she answered. "But may I have a cup of wine?"

So they drank together, and presently she said, "Who shall sing?"

"I will sing for you," replied Ishak.

"No," she said, "I have no mind for that tonight."

"Then will you sing yourself?"

"No," she said again. "I would like a fresh voice tonight. Go out and see if there is anyone in the street who would sing for us. I would like to hear a man of the people sing."

"There can be no one about in this dreadful weather," thought Ishak, but he opened the door, and looked up and down the street. To his surprise he saw an old beggar groping his way along by the wall and tapping with his stick.

Gathering his robe around him, Ishak splashed through the mud to the old man and said, "Are you a singer?"

"I am," answered the old man.

"Then will you join us and cheer us with your company?"

"Gladly," he said, "if you will take my hand and lead me to your house, for I am blind of both eyes."

Ishak led him in and bolted the door behind them, and Zayda welcomed him.

The old man ate a little, and washed his hands. Ishak gave him wine and he drank three cupfuls. Then he said, "Who are you?"

"I am Ishak-bin-Ibrahim of Mosul, my friend."

"I have heard of you, the sweet singer," the old man said. "I rejoice to be in your company. O Ishak, will you sing and play to me?"

Jokingly Ishak answered, "I hear and I obey." He took his lute and sang one of his sweetest songs, while Zayda listened in delight.

"Ah," said the old man, nodding his head. "You are almost a good singer."

Too disgusted to speak, Ishak laid down his lute without a word, and the old man went on, "Will the lady sing to us?"

Reluctantly Zayda took up the lute, and sang in the soft, clear voice which Ishak loved to hear.

When she had finished the old man nodded again. "You have shown no art, in singing or in playing."

Zayda flung the lute across the room in fury, and Ishak said angrily, "Now, will *you* sing?"

"I will sing with pleasure," the beggar answered, "if you will give me a new lute which has never been played before."

Silently Ishak went to the chest in which he kept his musical instruments, took out a new lute, and without speaking put it into the blind man's hands.

The old man tuned it carefully and sang, while Ishak listened with growing wonder and awe. Never in his life had he heard such singing. "Truly," he said to himself, "this man, this ragged old blind beggar, must be the greatest singer in the world."

When the song ended Ishak was too moved to speak. He rose and went to the table, and Zayda went with him. They filled three cups with wine. Then they turned to speak to the singer—and they stood dumbfounded. The old man was not there. He had vanished.

Ishak tried the door. It was still locked and bolted on the inside. He searched the house. Every door was securely fastened on the inside, every window was shuttered and barred.

Who was he, that wonderful singer who had come out of the night?

The Monkey Man

MAHMOOD's father was a very poor man who earned his bread by selling water in Cairo. He had a large bag made of an animal's skin which he filled with water at a well and carried on his back. He sprinkled water in front of shops and large houses to lay the dust, and collected a few small coins for doing it.

When he died he left the water bag to Mahmood, who found it too heavy to carry. He was not as strong as his father. So he sold the water bag and became a dervish, a holy man who wandered about and begged enough money to buy himself bread and sometimes a few dates or figs.

One day a rich lord gave him five silver dinars, and he was so hungry that he made up his mind to spend all this money on one very good meal. But on his way to the market he found a crowd watching a monkey. Its owner had it on a long chain. It jumped about, holding out its paws for nuts and money and making funny faces. All the crowd were laughing at it. But Mahmood did not laugh. It seemed as though a voice were saying to him, "Buy this monkey! You must buy this monkey! It will make your fortune!"

So he waited until all the crowd had gone. Then he said to the monkey's owner, "Will you sell me this monkey for three silver dinars?"

"It cost me ten dinars," replied the man, "but you may have it for eight."

"Four," said Mahmood.

"Seven," said the man.

"Four and a half," said Mahmood.

"Five," said the man, "and that is my last word. Pray for the prophet of Allah, my friend."

"Peace be upon him," answered Mahmood. He handed over his five dinars and led the monkey away.

He had nowhere to go except to a broken-down, empty house in a side street, where he sometimes slept. He was very hungry, but he had no money to buy supper for himself or the monkey. He sat down among the broken bricks, thinking of all the delicious food he could have bought with those five dinars, and wondering what to do.

Then the monkey began to shake itself in a very queer way, and suddenly it turned into a good-looking young man, dressed in fine clothes. Mahmood could hardly believe his eyes.

"O Mahmood," said the monkey man, "you have spent all your money on me, and now you cannot think of any way of getting us something to eat."

"That is true," answered Mahmood. "But who are you? Where do you come from, and what do you want?"

"Not so many questions!" the monkey man said, smiling. "Instead of asking me questions, take this gold dinar and go and buy us good food."

Mahmood went off to the market at once, and soon came back with the finest food he had ever had in his life. Together they ate it all, and then they lay down on the earthen floor to sleep. Mahmood covered the monkey man with his ragged old cloak to keep him warm.

Next morning the man woke Mahmood and said, "One night on the bare ground is enough. Go now and rent for us a fine palace in the city, and furnish it as splendidly as you can."

He gave Mahmood a large bag of gold, and in a few hours they had one of the most splendid palaces in Cairo.

"Now, Mahmood," said the youth, "are you not ashamed to be so dirty and ragged? You can have more money now than all the kings of the earth. Here is gold. Buy the most splendid clothes in Cairo, go to the hammam, the public bathhouse, and get rid of these old rags forever."

You may be sure that Mahmood lost no time about it, and when he came back he looked like a prince, for he was a handsome young man.

"Ah," said the monkey man, "that is better. Now, how would you like to have the Sultan's daughter for your wife? She is more beautiful than the fairest moon that ever shone in a cloudless sky."

"O my master," answered Mahmood, bowing very low, "nothing could please me more."

"Then take this packet of jewels, go to the Sultan, and ask

for his eldest daughter in marriage. It is written that you shall marry her, and the Sultan will see that you are her rightful lord."

So Mahmood presented himself at the Sultan of Cairo's magnificent palace. The guards thought he was a great prince, and when he said that he had a present for the Sultan, they led him at once to the throne room.

The Sultan sat on a throne of gold, under a canopy of the finest green silk, with richly dressed lords and captains about him. But Mahmood was not afraid. He bowed low before the Sultan and gave him the packet of jewels. "O King," he said, "I beg you to accept this humble gift."

The Sultan told the Grand Wazir, his chief minister, to open the packet, and when he saw the magnificent jewels which it contained he marveled. "Your gift is accepted," he cried. "Now tell me your desire. Kings are not backward in giving gifts."

"O Sultan of the age," said Mahmood, "if your mightiness will pardon me I ask a very rich gift. I ask for that hidden jewel, that precious pearl, your eldest daughter."

The Sultan looked at him hard and long, and at last he answered, "It is permitted to ask."

He turned to the Grand Wazir and said, "What do you think of this noble lord's demand?"

"The answer is in his face," replied the Wazir. "He is surely not unworthy of the Princess. But it might be well to test him."

"What do you suggest?" asked the Sultan.

"O King," replied the Wazir, "I suggest that you show

him the largest, finest diamond in your treasury and ask him for one of equal value."

Mahmood was full of fear at this, but he did not show it. "My lord," he said, "may I indeed have your daughter in marriage on that condition?"

"You may," said the Sultan.

Then he sent for his largest diamond. "Look well at it," he said. "If you bring me a diamond just like this, she shall be yours."

Mahmood took the great jewel in his hand and looked at it very carefully. He gave it to the Wazir and bowed very low to the Sultan. "If it is permitted," he said, "I shall come back tomorrow."

Then he took his leave gracefully.

When the monkey man had heard Mahmood's story, he said, "It shall be done. But it cannot be done tonight."

Next morning he went out into the garden very early and after an hour he came back into the palace with ten diamonds, every one of them exactly like the Sultan's diamond. They filled the room with light.

Mahmood marveled more than ever at the monkey man's magic powers. But he lost no time. He set out at once for the Sultan's palace, carrying the diamonds in a little jeweled casket. The monkey man went with him.

Mahmood stood before the throne, bowed low, and said, "O King, O Sultan of the age, I beg to be excused. I could not find one diamond that was good enough, so I have brought ten. I beg you, my lord, to accept any of these which may please you and to throw the rest away."

Then he opened the little casket, and the Sultan fell back
on his throne in astonishment. He could not speak. He looked
at his Grand Wazir, who said, "My lord, surely he should
have the Princess."

The marriage was soon arranged and the marriage papers

were drawn up. Since Mahmood could not read, the monkey man took him aside and read them to him.

"Now," said the monkey man, "there is one thing I want you to do for me."

"I will do anything," answered Mahmood. "I owe everything to you."

"When you are left alone with your bride tonight you will see that she has a silver bracelet on her right arm. Get her to give it to you, and then bring it to me at once. Then you can go back to her."

The wedding was celebrated with great rejoicing, feasting and singing, music and fireworks. It went on for hours. At last Mahmood took his beautiful bride to his own palace, where she was much impressed by the magnificence of it all.

"Now," said Mahmood, "I want to ask something from you. Will you give me this silver bracelet?"

"Why, yes," she answered in surprise. "All I have is yours. This is a holy bracelet which my nurse gave me when I was a child. I have worn it ever since. But here it is."

He took it from her, kissed her between the eyes, and said, "I must leave you, but only for a moment."

He hurried off to find the monkey man, who was waiting in the great hall, and gave him the bracelet.

There was a crash of thunder, and then darkness. The palace and everything about him vanished. Mahmood found himself lying on the earth, in the ruins of the house where he and the monkey man had spent their first night. His splendid clothes had vanished too. He was wearing his filthy old rags.

There he lay in misery all that night. Next day he wandered about the streets, begging a few small coins to buy something to eat. He did not know what to do.

Presently he came upon a Moor from the land of Barbary, who was sitting on a mat in a side street. In front of him was a small carpet, and on it were laid books of magic and things by which he foretold what would happen in the future.

Mahmood had never seen him before, but he looked at Mahmood with eyes like swords and said at once, "Are you not the young man who has lost his wife?"

"In Allah's name I am," answered Mahmood.

"Oh, unhappy man," said the Moor. "The monkey which you bought for five dinars is not human at all. He is a very wicked Jinnee, an evil spirit. He used you to get what he wanted. He has wanted the Sultan's daughter for a long time, but he could not go near her so long as she was wearing that bracelet, for it is holy. As soon as you had taken it from her he carried her off to his secret cave in the desert."

"Alas, alas," cried Mahmood, "I shall never see her again and I shall be a beggar all my days." He threw himself down on the ground and wept.

"Do not give up hope," said the Moor. "I will try to right your wrongs. This Jinnee has done many wicked things among the true believers who worship Allah. We must make an end."

Mahmood looked up at him hopefully. He took a scroll of parchment from his carpet and said, "Mahmood, take this, and walk into the desert, toward the setting sun, for a day and a night. Then wait. A troop of beings will pass. Give this scroll to him who seems to be their chief. We shall see what we shall see."

"I hear and obey," answered Mahmood. "I thank you most humbly with all my heart." He bowed very low and set out upon his journey.

He walked for a day and a night, and then he came to a place of wild grass, where he found dates to eat and a spring of water. He sat down to wait. He heard thousands of birds

all around him. He heard their wings, but he could see nothing. He was full of fear, but he waited.

Then night fell, and soon he saw a great number of torches which came quickly nearer and began to pass him by. They were carried by invisible hands. No one was to be seen until at last there came, moving through the air, a litter of silver on which was a throne of gold. On the throne sat a King, dressed in splendid scarlet robes. On his head was a crown of jewels which shone with a thousand points of light.

As he passed by, the King looked long at Mahmood, who tried to speak and could not. He was so full of fear that his tongue stuck to the roof of his mouth and his knees knocked together.

The King made a sign with his hand, and the unseen bearers of the litter came to a stand. His eyes were still fixed on Mahmood, who knelt and kissed the ground between his hands. Then the King said, "Where is the writing from my friend, the Barbary Moor?"

"It is here, O King," answered Mahmood, taking the scroll from the front of his robe. He went forward on his knees and gave it to the King.

The King read the scroll. Then he cried to an invisible someone, "O Atrash, go swiftly and bring me the Jinnee who lives in the cave of fire. Bring him in chains."

There was a short silence. All the torches stood still. Then there was a clanking of chains, and unseen hands dragged the monkey man before the King. His wrists and ankles were chained together. He had a man's body still, but now his head was a monkey's head. He was howling like a dog.

"Why have you done this evil thing?" cried the King. "How dare you steal the Princess?"

"She's mine. I shall keep her," howled the monkey man.

"You cannot keep her if you give up the silver bracelet. Give it back to this human, or we shall talk together."

"Never!" howled the monkey man. "Never! Never!"

He opened his mouth wide. His throat was full of flaming fire, like a furnace. With his chained hands he plucked the silver bracelet from the front of his robe and threw it into the depths of his throat.

The King stretched out his right hand. His arm grew longer and longer until it was three times the length of a human arm. With one blow he struck the monkey man dead and flung him to the earth.

"O Atrash," said the King, "take the bracelet from his throat and give it back to this human."

Mahmood took the bracelet from the unseen hands which offered it to him. As he took it the King, the torches, the desert vanished into darkness. A great wind swept him away. A moment later he found himself in his splendid palace in Cairo. He was dressed in his princely robes again and his beautiful bride stood beside him. He put the silver bracelet on her arm.

They lived in peace and happiness together all their days, and when the old Sultan died Mahmood reigned in his place.

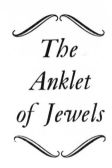

The
Anklet
of Jewels

AMONG other sayings it is said that there were once, in an old city, three sisters who lived together. They earned their bread by spinning flax into thread. All three were as beautiful as a full moon in a clear sky. But the two elder sisters were mean and spiteful, while the youngest, whose name was Yasmeen, was kindhearted and altogether charming. So her sisters were very jealous of her.

One day she went to the market and sold her thread at a good price. Then she bought a lovely little pot, with which she was very pleased. She took it home to her bedroom and put a red rose in it.

"Isn't it pretty?" she said to her sisters.

"No, I think it's ugly," snapped the eldest.

"*And* a shocking waste of money," said the second sister.

Then they too went off to the market to sell their thread.

Yasmeen took up the little pot in both hands and stroked it lovingly.

"How beautiful it is!" she said to herself. "How I wish I had a dress as beautiful as this little pot!"

At once a robe of silk floated down from the air and unseen hands laid it across her knees.

"Oh," she gasped. "This is magic! This must be a magic pot!"

She picked up the robe and unfolded it gently. It was of the finest pale blue silk, trimmed with sapphires and diamonds. It was the loveliest thing that Yasmeen had ever seen. Quickly she took off her plain cotton frock and put on her new dress. Then she walked about the room, looking at herself in her little mirror, loving the soft touch of the silk, the faint rustle of its folds. The room seemed full of sunshine.

Suddenly she stopped short. "I'm hungry," she said to herself. "I wonder—I wonder if the magic pot would give me something to eat."

She took it up in her hands and whispered to it, "Little pot, little pot, I wish I had something very nice to eat."

The unseen hands covered her table with a fine cloth of embroidered linen, and set down on it a large silver dish full of the most delicious sweetmeats: jellies, jams, honey, cakes, tarts, and a jug of iced sherbet. She had never tasted anything so delicious.

She was just finishing the sweetmeats when she heard her sisters coming home. Quickly she wished away the tablecloth, the silver dish, and the silk dress, and went downstairs to her spinning wheel.

She did not dare tell her sisters about the magic pot; she was sure they would take it away from her. But when they were out of the house or were fast asleep in bed, she wished herself dresses, jewels, beautiful flowers, delicious food, and many other things. Afterward she wished them away again —except for the food!

One day the Sultan of that city arranged a great feast for the twenty-first birthday of his eldest son, the Prince Yusef, and heralds went through every street, blowing their trumpets and inviting everyone to the feast.

When the day came the elder sisters put on their best clothes, and went off to the palace, telling Yasmeen that she must stay at home to look after the house.

No sooner had they gone, however, than Yasmeen went to her room and said, "Little pot, little pot, I wish to be the fairest of the fair at the Sultan's feast tonight. I wish for the most beautiful clothes and jewels in the world!"

The unseen hands heaped the jewels on her table and laid the clothes gently across her bed. Quickly she put them on; a long dress of green silk, a red waistcoat, a white mantle, and an embroidered green veil which covered her face up to her eyes. All were of the most delicate and beautiful silk that the silkworms of China had ever made. She slipped her little feet into silver shoes. Then she put on the jewels. She braided her hair with a long string of little diamonds and emeralds which seemed to dance in the light. She put on a splendid necklace of diamonds worth more than a king's crown. She clasped golden bracelets on both her wrists, and golden anklets set with diamonds and emeralds on her slender ankles. When she looked in the mirror she hoped that perhaps she would be indeed the fairest of the fair.

Prince Yusef was a very handsome, charming young man, but if Yasmeen had hoped to catch a glimpse of him she was disappointed. The men and women were kept separate as usual, and the Queen was feasting the women in her own apartment. There Yasmeen lowered her veil, and the guests were so struck by her beauty that they gathered around her, and found her as charming and modest as she was beautiful. She looked so different from her everyday self that no one, not even her sisters, recognized her. The Queen noticed her, and when the feast began she was given a place at the Queen's table.

She had never been so happy before, and only one thing troubled her; how was she to make sure of getting home before her sisters did? But when the feast was over, and palace maidens stood up to sing and dance for the guests' delight, Yasmeen was able to slip away while the Queen was watching the dancers.

She was in such a hurry, however, that she went out by the wrong door, into the stableyard. In the dark she caught her foot against a horse trough and lost one of her anklets, but she did not dare stop and look for it. She hurried home, and when her two sisters arrived she was in her cotton dress, working at her spinning wheel.

Next morning Prince Yusef thought he would like to go for a ride on his favorite pony, and he went out to the stables. The grooms were just trying to water the horses, but when they led a horse to the trough it would not drink; it snorted, and stamped and drew back. Nothing the grooms could do was of any use. The Prince went to see what was the matter.

He saw something which glittered at the bottom of the trough, and when he took it out he found to his astonishment that it was an anklet of gold richly set with precious stones.

Suddenly his fingers tingled, and a strange feeling shot through him. He took the anklet to the Sultan.

"O my lord and father," he said, "you told me yesterday that you wanted me to marry. It may be that I have found a bride." He showed the anklet to the Sultan and told him how he had found it. "Surely," he said, "a maiden with an ankle so slim as this must be beautiful."

"Surely," said the Sultan, "she must be the daughter of a great lord. Any one of the jewels in this anklet is worth more than all the jewels in my crown."

"I will marry her!" cried the Prince.

"Well, as to that, my son," said the Sultan, "do you go and talk to the Queen your mother. She will know better than I what is best to be done."

Off he went to the Queen, who recognized the anklet at once.

"Why," she cried, "this belongs to a maiden who came to the feast last night. No one knew her, but she won all our hearts. I would have asked her after the feast who she was and whence she came, but she had disappeared."

"O my lady and my mother," said the Prince, "I beg you to find her for me. She has taken hold of my heart!"

The Queen sent her herald through the city to find the owner of the anklet. He went first to the houses of the great lords and the rich merchants, but none of their daughters had ankles slim enough. He went on from house to house, until he reached that of the three sisters.

"The anklet is mine," said Yasmeen, and slipped it on, while her sisters stared in amazement.

The herald bowed to her. "Fair lady," he said, "the Queen has commanded me to lead you to her."

"I will come in a moment," answered Yasmeen. Going up to her room she wished for the green robe, the white mantle, and the other anklet which she had worn at the feast. Then she went with the herald, leaving her sisters so astonished that they could not speak.

When she came into the Queen's presence she knelt and bowed her forehead to the ground. But the Queen raised her up and embraced her and said, "My sweet child, I am happy to see you again."

She sent word to Prince Yusef, who came in great haste. The Queen commanded Yasmeen to unveil her face, and she blushed and did so, for she could not disobey the Queen. Yusef was so amazed at her beauty that he threw himself at her feet, and as for Yasmeen, she thought him the most charming young man she had ever seen.

You may be sure that it was not long before the marriage was arranged and the wedding day fixed, with grand celebrations of all kinds. Yasmeen wished herself more and more beautiful dresses and jewels for her sisters and herself to wear at the wedding, so she had to tell them the secret of the little pot. They made a wicked plan, for they were more jealous of her than ever. One day, when Yasmeen was out, they asked the little pot to give them a magic pin, which it did.

When the wedding day came they helped Yasmeen to dress in her finest robes. Then they pushed the magic pin into her hair, and at once she was changed into a dove. They tried to catch the bird, but she flew out of the window and disappeared.

Then the two wicked sisters ran to the palace, weeping and tearing their hair, and told the Prince that Yasmeen had gone out of the house and not come back. No one had seen where she went and they could not find her anywhere. "Alas, alas," they moaned, "our dear sister! She was so happy, and now she has vanished away!"

The Prince was heartbroken. The Sultan's guards and the Queen's women searched every house in the city, and every village nearby, but no trace of Yasmeen could be found.

Prince Yusef lay miserably in his chamber, getting nothing but bad news every day. But every morning a beautiful white dove perched outside his window, crooning very sadly. When this had gone on for a week he opened the window, and the dove flew into the room. He held out his hand, and to his surprise the dove perched on it, rubbing her feathers lovingly against his fingers.

He stroked the dove gently, until presently he felt something hard under the feathers.

"Little dove," he said, "what is this?"

She crooned again, turning her head so that he could see what he had found. When he parted the feathers he saw the large head of a pin. He pulled. It came out in his hand—and in a moment the dove had become his beautiful bride.

You can guess how happy they were then! The wedding was celebrated that very day, amid the greatest rejoicings.

When the two wicked sisters heard the news they were so angry that they fell down dead, but Prince Yusef and Princess Yasmeen lived happily ever afterwards. The little magic pot gave them anything they needed, and Allah blessed them with many beautiful children.

The
Dream
Treasure

IN THE beautiful city of Baghdad there was once a man whose name was Bekkar. He had many ships which sailed to other lands, and brought back goods for him to sell in Baghdad. They brought silks and linens, sweet perfumes, precious jewels, monkeys and peacocks, and many other things.

Bekkar and his family lived in a fine house which was well known in Baghdad because it had tall black marble pillars beside the main doorway. They were a happy family until their troubles began. Some of his ships were wrecked on rocks, some were taken by pirates, and some sank in storms at sea.

One day the news came that the last of his ships had been sunk, and he knew he was ruined. He had no money left, and he sat all day beside the beautiful fountain in his courtyard, sadly wondering what he should do. He could not think of anything.

That night he dreamed a strange dream. An old man appeared to him in his dream, an old, old man with white hair and a long white beard, dressed like an Arab who lived in the desert. The old man said, "Bekkar, you must go to Cairo, and there you will find good fortune." Then he vanished.

Next day Bekkar thought this over, but he could not see any sense in it, so he did nothing.

On the second night the old man appeared to him again and said, "Bekkar, you must go to Cairo, and there you will find good fortune." But Bekkar did nothing about it.

On the third night he dreamed the same dream. The old man came to him and said, "Bekkar, I tell you for the last time, you must go to Cairo, and there you will find good fortune. I shall not come again." And he vanished in a cloud of smoke.

Next day Bekkar told his wife about his dream. "Oh," she said, "if you have dreamed this three times you must do what the old man told you to do. You must go to Cairo. You cannot be worse off than you are now, and I believe your dream will come true."

"But it's a long, dangerous journey," he said, "and I have no money."

"Borrow money from your friends," she answered. "Give me some of it so that we do not starve while you are away, and go to Cairo at once. It is our only hope."

So Bekkar did as she said. He bought a camel to ride, and dates and figs and other things to eat. Then he set out with a caravan to make the long journey across the desert. When at last they reached Cairo he had not enough money to stay at a khan, an inn, but he left his camel at one, and went to a mosque, where the Arabs worshiped their god, Allah. There

he lay down in a dark corner on the stone floor and was soon
fast asleep.

Now next door to this mosque there was the house of a
very rich man, and that night a gang of thieves broke into it.
The owner heard them and called his slaves, who drove them
out of the house and chased them. The thieves ran through
the mosque and woke Bekkar, who sprang to his feet and
was so startled that he too began to run. The slaves caught
him, while all the thieves got away. They thought he was
one of the thieves. They beat him till he could hardly stand,
then they dragged him away and threw him into prison.

Next morning he was taken before the judge, who heard
all that the rich man's slaves had to say and all that Bekkar had
to say. He believed Bekkar's story, and set him free.

"Now, tell me," said the judge, "why you, a merchant of
Baghdad, have come to Cairo?"

"Because of a dream I had," answered Bekkar sadly.
"Three times an old man appeared to me in my sleep and
told me that if I came to Cairo I should find good fortune.
But all I have got is a beating from these men."

The judge laughed and laughed. "Well!" he cried. "If you
are foolish enough to believe in a dream you deserve a beating! I have dreamed three times that in your city of Baghdad
there is a house with pillars of black marble beside the door,
and in the courtyard of this house there is a beautiful fountain, and beside the fountain a great treasure is buried. But
do you think I am going to Baghdad to look for a house I've
seen in a dream? I'm not such a fool! And you, my friend,
you go home and learn wisdom. And peace go with you."

Bekkar bowed low and went quickly, for the house in the judge's dream must be his own house. He got his camel from the khan and rode as fast as he could to Baghdad. As soon as he reached home he took a spade and dug beside the fountain. There he found a large chest full of diamonds, rubies, emeralds, sapphires, and pearls. They were worth a fortune, and Bekkar and his family lived happily ever afterward.

The
Black
Door

LONG years ago, in an Arabian city, a young man was sitting against a wall in the marketplace. He was hungry, dirty, ragged, and very miserable because he had wasted all his money. His name was Ahmad. He was sitting there hoping that someone would give him work to do.

Presently an old man with a long gray beard and a sad face came along.

"My boy," he said, "do you want work?"

"I do indeed," answered Ahmad. He stood up and bowed. "I am starving."

"I can see by your face," said the old man, "that you are no ordinary beggar. I need a young man to take charge of my house and my servants and look after me. Will you do this? If we get on happily together you shall be well housed, well fed, and well paid."

"To hear is to obey," said Ahmad joyfully, and he bowed again.

The old man took him to the hammam, the public bathhouse, and sent a servant to get a fine linen robe for him. When Ahmad came out he was no longer a dirty beggar dressed in rags but a good-looking and charming young man.

They went to the old man's house, which was large and beautiful. It was built around a central courtyard, with a rose garden in the middle of it and a fountain which splashed like music to the ear. All the rooms looked into this garden. The rooms were built of many-colored marbles, their ceilings were wonderfully painted in gold and bright colors, and there were rich, soft carpets on the floors. There were white servants and Negro servants, wearing blue and silver liveries, and clever cooks in the large kitchen.

"You shall take charge of it all," said the old man. "Here is a bag containing fifty gold dinars. When they are gone tell me how you have spent them, and I will give you more. I have no wife and no children. I hope you will be like a son to me. But there is one condition. If you find me weeping, you must never ask me why."

"I hear and I obey," said Ahmad very gladly, and all went well. He had been used to a large house of his own, so he knew how things should be done. He often found the old man weeping bitterly. But he never asked him why.

Years passed and the two got on very well together. Then one day the old man was taken ill. He knew that his time had come to die. He sent for Ahmad and said, "My son, you have always been kind and faithful to me. Now I must say goodbye, for I am passing out of this world into the mercy of God. I leave to you this house, all my money, and everything I have. Here are my keys. There is one warning I must give you; do not open the black door, or your life may be made as unhappy as mine has been. I have forgotten how to laugh. I did not keep my promise. I broke my word."

He turned his face to the wall and died.

Ahmad was very sorry, and built a splendid tomb for him, and gave alms to all the poor people of the city in his memory.

For three months Ahmad lived happily enough in that beautiful house. Then one day he suddenly remembered what the old man had said about the black door.

"Where can it be?" he asked himself. "I have never noticed it."

He searched and searched until he found it, in a very dark corner of a passage which was not used. There were spiders' webs across the door, and it was fastened with three steel padlocks.

He stood and looked at it. "Well," he said to himself, "there it is, and the old man warned me not to open it." So he went away.

But he could not forget the door. For seven days he thought about it, and for seven nights he dreamed about it.

"No," he cried at last, "I must open it!"

He tried all the keys until he opened the door. There was only a narrow passage, winding away into the darkness. After fetching a torch he walked along the passage. He walked for three hours, and then suddenly found himself on a sea beach which he had never seen before.

He walked down the beach and stood looking at the wide, empty blue sea. Suddenly an enormous bird swooped down, took him up in its great claws, and carried him out to sea.

For an hour it flew on, and this seemed like many hours to Ahmad, but at last the bird put him down on a little island and flew away.

Ahmad walked all around the island. There was nothing to eat, nothing to drink and no shelter, and the sun was very hot. "If I cannot get away soon," he said, "I shall die of hunger and thirst. But what can I do?"

Then he saw, far away, a ship like a star in the sky. He watched it anxiously. Would it come near enough to see him and rescue him, or would it pass by? The ship came nearer. Then he saw that it was heading straight for the island, and he was filled with joy.

Soon he could see that it was a wonderful little ship, built of ivory and ebony, inlaid with shining gold. The oars were made of precious sandalwood. The rowers were ten girls, all of them as beautiful as the moon in a cloudless sky.

They drove the ship onto the beach and sprang ashore. He hurried to meet them, and they crowded around him, kissing his hands in homage. Then an eleventh girl came from the ship, a girl even more beautiful and more beautifully dressed than the others. She too kissed Ahmad's hands. She carried a silken bag from which she took a royal robe of scarlet velvet, embroidered with diamonds. She put it on him, and all the girls bowed before him, crying, "O King of the age, O bridegroom of the princely bride, we salute you. We are your slaves."

Ahmad stood in a daze, thinking that he must be dreaming. He could not speak. He let them lead him aboard the ship, where they sat him in a chair of state, with a silken canopy

over him and rich carpets under his feet. The girls pushed
off the ship and rowed swiftly across the sea.

At last they came to land, to a fine harbor built of yellow
stone. Ahmad saw beyond it a splendid city, full of palaces
and minarets, gardens and trees; and at the harbor, waiting to
greet him, were guards in uniform, mounted on fine horses.
They saluted him with a great clash of their swords on their
shields. He rose from his chair of state, bowed to them, and
stepped ashore. He still felt that he must be dreaming. They
mounted him on a stately horse, richly caparisoned in cloth
of gold, and set out for the city, with drums beating and flags
fluttering in the breeze.

Soon they were riding on grass, among beds of bright
flowers, under trees which were full of singing birds. An
army came out from the city to meet them, and from its ranks
there rode forward a single horseman. He was a kingly figure
clad in flashing armor, with a jeweled crown on his head and
his face half-covered by a silken scarf.

The King dismounted, Ahmad too sprang from his horse,
and they greeted each other with courtly grace.

Then the King said, "You are my lord Ahmad, are you
not?"

"My name is Ahmad, O King of the age," he answered.

"Our books of magic have told us that you were coming,"
said the King. "You are our honored guest. Will you come
with me?"

"Most gladly, O King," he said. "I thank you with all my
heart."

So they mounted and rode on, stirrup touching stirrup, in

stately procession. Presently they came to the royal palace. There the King took Ahmad by the hand and led him into a magnificent marble throne room, where a throne of gold stood on a dais.

The King seated Ahmad on the throne and sat beside him. All the courtiers and officers and soldiers who filled the room bowed low before them both.

The King unwound the silk scarf from his face, and Ahmad saw to his astonishment that the "King" was in fact a lovely girl. She was so perfect in beauty that she seemed to fill the room with sunshine. Ahmad's heart stood still. Then it filled with joy, and from that moment he loved her.

She laid a hand gently on Ahmad's hand. "My King, my dear lord," she said, "you must know that I am the Queen of this land, and that all the guards and soldiers whom you have seen today are women. There is no man among them. In this kingdom the men are our servants, and work in the houses and fields. The women rule the land."

While Ahmad wondered at this, in came the Grand Wazir, the chief minister, who was a woman with long gray hair.

The Princess said to her, "O Wazir, bring the kazi, the royal lawyer." The Wazir bowed low and went away.

The Queen turned and smiled at Ahmad, dazzling him again with her beauty.

"My lord Ahmad," she said, "it is written that you shall be our King. Will you take this throne to be yours? Will you take me to be your wife?"

He threw himself on his knees before her. "My Queen, my dear lady," he cried, "I am your slave forever."

"Not so," she said. "You shall be my lord and king." She raised him and kissed him between the eyes and made him take his place again beside her on the throne. "All my officers and servants shall be your officers and servants. This palace shall be yours, and everything in it. There is only one condition."

She looked at him very seriously.

"I will do anything you ask," he said.

"You see that black door at the end of the hall?"

"I see it," he answered.

"Will you swear to me that you will never open that door?"

"By the name of God," he said, "I swear that I will never, never open that door."

The kazi came, and Ahmad and the Princess were married. She took the crown from her head and placed it on his.

Then all the great ladies cried, "Long live King Ahmad! Long live the King!" and they all kissed his hands in homage and swore to be his loyal servants.

Seven years passed, and Ahmad and the Queen were happy together. But he left the ruling of the kingdom to the Wazir and the other officers and often he had little to do.

One day when he was alone and bored he remembered the black door. He went to the the throne room. There was no one else there. He stood looking at the door.

"There must be something very wonderful behind it," he said to himself. "It was the black door in my own house which led me to this magic kingdom. I have kept my promise long enough."

He opened the door.

Behind it there was darkness and the great bird which had carried him to the island.

He turned and ran. In one swoop the bird overtook him, caught him up in its terrible claws, and flew out of the palace up into the sky.

On it flew, on and on, until at last it set him down on the beach from which it had first taken him up seven years before. Then it flew away.

Ahmad knew that there was no hope for him. He found the passage and went back slowly and sadly to his own house. There he lived for the rest of his days, thinking of the lovely wife and the wonderful kingdom he had lost, and, like the old man he had served, he never laughed again.

The
Queen
of the
Serpents

IN THE land of the Sultan Karazdan there lived once an old Greek named Daniel who was so wise that he became famous as a teacher and a healer, and men came from far and near to sit at his feet and learn from him.

When he died he left a baby son named Hassib Karim al-Din, whose mother brought him up very carefully, hoping that he might become as wise as his father. She sent him to school when he was five, and then to other schools, but it was no good; he seemed unable to learn. After he left school it was just as bad; there was nothing he could do well. In despair his mother married him to a beautiful girl, whom she chose with great care, hoping that a good wife would make a man of him. But he went on being a hopeless dunce.

Then some of the widow's neighbors who were woodcutters came to her and said, "If you will buy an ax and ropes and a donkey for Hassib we will take him with us to the forest and make a woodcutter of him." The widow agreed, and after this Hassib was kept hard at work. He sold his wood

in the market and earned enough money to keep his wife
and mother.

This went on for some time, until one day there was a
great storm of rain. The woodcutters took shelter in a cave,
where Hassib sat hitting the earth idly with his ax. To his
surprise it sounded hollow. He dug for a little, and found an
iron ring let into a large flat stone, so he called the others and
together they heaved up the stone. They were astonished to
discover under it a great tank lined with wood and full of
the finest honey.

"Now Allah be praised," cried one. "This honey will
fetch a high price in the market. Let us go and get jars to
carry it."

So they left Hassib to guard the honey and went to the
city, where they bought large earthenware jars which they
lashed to their donkeys' saddles. They told no one their
secret, and for five days they sold honey, making a great
profit.

On the sixth day, when the honey was nearly all gone, one
of them who had an evil mind whispered to his fellows, "Hassib found this honey. When we go home he will go to the
Kadi, the Judge, and claim that all the money should be his,
and the Kadi may agree. Now let us lower Hassib into the
pit to get the last of the honey. Then we can leave him there
and he will die."

They all agreed to this wicked plan, and when they
reached the cave they said to Hassib, "This is your honey,
and we want to get all of it for your sake. Let us lower you
into the pit and you can bale it out to the very last drop."

He agreed, and when the last jar had been hauled up he called to them, "Now let down a rope and haul me up." But they took no notice. They loaded their donkeys with the honey jars and rode away.

After they had sold the honey they went together to Hassib's mother, weeping and wringing their hands, and they said to her, "May Allah grant that you long outlive your son!"

Then the poor woman burst into tears and called Hassib's wife, and they wept together.

"What happened to him?" asked his mother.

The leader answered, "We were cutting wood on the mountaintop when it began to rain. We took refuge in a cave, with our donkeys, but Hassib's donkey broke loose and galloped down the mountain. Hassib ran after it and a large wolf sprang upon him out of a thicket. We ran to scare away the wolf but we were too late. Hassib was dead. We buried him where he lay. Alas! Alas!" And all the wicked wood-cutters wept again, and went away, leaving the two women to mourn, beating their breasts and casting dust on their heads.

Meanwhile Hassib was in a sad state, for it was impossible for him to get out of the pit. He wept and wailed and cried, "There is no majesty and no might save in Allah, the Compassionate, the Merciful!"

Suddenly a little snake appeared on the wall of the pit, and fell at his feet. He crushed it before it could bite him, and then he said to himself, "How did the snake get in?"

He searched the wall and found a long crack in the wood, and when he put his eye to the crack he saw a faint distant glimmer of light. Drawing his woodman's knife from his belt he hacked away at the crack, until he had made a hole large enough for him to squeeze through.

He found himself in what seemed to be a large cave, quite dark except for the light in the distance. So he walked very cautiously toward it until he came to a long gallery, brightly lit. This led him to a huge door of black iron, closed by a silver padlock in which there was a golden key. The sun was shining through a crack in the door. He unlocked it and found himself in a beautiful green valley full of sunshine.

In the valley was a lake which shimmered like silver, and on a green hill beside it stood a golden throne studded with precious stones which flashed brilliantly in the sun. Around the throne were set hundreds of stools, some of gold, some of silver, some of emerald. Hassib was now very tired. He sat on the throne and looked about him, marveling, until presently he fell asleep.

Suddenly he was awakened by a terrible noise. Then he saw that on every stool there was now coiled a large serpent, which looked at him with eyes blazing like live coals, and hissed. Hassib was terrified; he thought his last hour had come.

At that moment the waters of the lake parted and there rose out of them a serpent, larger than any of the others, which carried on its head a tray of gold. In the tray was a shining serpent with the face of a beautiful girl, who wore on her head a crown of diamonds.

All the serpents prostrated themselves on the earth in homage to her, and Hassib, quickly leaving the throne, did the same. The great serpent carried her up the hill and set her on the golden throne. She looked at Hassib, who trembled before her, but she said to him, "Have no fear of us, O youth. I am the Queen of the Serpents, and none of them will harm you." Hassib prostrated himself again, kissing the earth in front of her. "You are welcome to my kingdom," she went on. "What is your name?"

"I am called Hassib Karim al-Din," he answered.

Then she bade one of the serpents bring him food, and the serpent brought a silver tray loaded with apples and grapes, walnuts, almonds, and bananas, which he ate eagerly, for he was very hungry, and he gave thanks to Allah.

When he had eaten his fill the Queen said to him, "Tell me, O Hassib, how you found your way here from the land of men. Tell me all your adventures."

"To hear is to obey," he answered, and when he had finished his story the Queen said, "Now I will tell you my own story."

She told him a very strange tale, she showed him all the wonders of her kingdom, and the time passed happily for Hassib. Two years went by as though they were two days, but then he felt a great longing to see his wife and mother and his own country again. Going to the Queen, he prostrated himself and asked her permission to return.

"I will let you go, O Hassib," she said, "if you will do one thing. You must promise me that you will never go again to the hammam, the public bathhouse, for if you do, great evil will befall us both."

"This I promise," he answered.

"But I am afraid," she went on, "that when you are back in your own country you will forget your promise."

"Never!" he cried. "I swear by the name of Allah, the Compassionate, the Merciful, that I will never enter the hammam again so long as I live."

At this the Queen was satisfied. She commanded one of her great serpents to carry Hassib back to a place near the cave in which he had found the honey. Thence he walked to the city, and by the last of the day, the yellowing of the sun, he came to his own house and knocked at the door.

His mother opened it. She gave a great cry, she threw her arms around him and wept for joy. His wife hurried to the door, and she greeted him, weeping and kissing his hands. They went together joyfully into the house, where Hassib told them his story. Then he asked his mother about the woodcutters who had left him to die.

She answered, "They told us that a wolf had killed you, and we bewailed you as dead. As for them, they have become rich merchants, and own houses and shops, and the world goes well with them. But every day they send me meat and drink which are enough for us both."

"Tomorrow," he said, "do you go to them and say, 'My son, Hassib Karim al-Din, has returned from his travels. Come and salute him and bid him welcome home!' "

This she did, at which the woodcutters gathered together, and each of them gave her a robe of fine silk embroidered with gold, saying, "Give these to your good son and tell him we will visit him tomorrow."

Then the woodcutters called in some merchants who were friends of theirs and after telling them the whole story they asked what they should do, for they were afraid.

"If Hassib takes his case to the Kadi," said the oldest merchant, "it will go hard with you. The best thing would be for each of you to give Hassib half his wealth, and ask for his pardon."

They all agreed with this, so next morning all the woodcutters, carrying purses of gold coins and bags of precious jewels, went to Hassib's house, saluted him, and humbly kissed his hands. Then they laid before him all the riches they had brought, and said, "We submit ourselves to your mercy."

He accepted their peace offerings and replied, "That which is past is past. That which happened was the will of Allah."

They all thanked him in turn and said, "Now let us rejoice together. Let us walk about the city, and go to the hammam."

"That I cannot do," he said. "I have taken a solemn oath never to visit the baths again as long as I live."

"Then come to our houses so that we can feast together."

He agreed to this, and each of them in turn entertained him royally for a night and a day, after which Hassib set up as a merchant, for he too was now a rich man.

All went well with him, and with his wife and his mother until one day he passed a hammam whose keeper knew him well. This keeper, standing at the door of the bathhouse, saluted him, and embraced him, saying, "Favor me by entering the bath, and there wash and be massaged. You will be much refreshed, for my slaves are skillful, and I shall be glad to have you as my guest."

"I thank you," answered Hassib, "but I cannot accept for I have sworn never to enter a hammam again."

The keeper flew into a passion. He called to his slaves, who seized Hassib, dragged him into the bathhouse in spite of his cries, pulled off his clothes, and forced him into the bath. But they had hardly begun to pour water on his head when three men who were seated by the bath rose up and said to him, "You must come to the Sultan. He has great need of you."

They sent a messenger at once to the Sultan's chief minister, the Wazir, who came in haste to the hammam, bringing a company of the Sultan's guards. Going to Hassib he saluted him, saying, "Welcome, welcome!" Then he mounted Hassib on a horse, and hurried him to the palace of the Sultan Karazdan.

Here he seated Hassib comfortably in a rich chamber, and called for the finest food and wine to be set before them. When they had eaten and washed their hands theWazir clad him in two robes of honor, each of them worth five thousand dinars, and said to him, "Allah has been merciful to us in sending you, O Son of Daniel, for the Sultan is dying of leprosy, and our books of wisdom tell us that only you can cure him."

Then he called together a host of princes and courtiers, and they accompanied Hassib through the seven great doors to the Sultan's chamber.

Now the Sultan Karazdan was one of the greatest monarchs on earth, King of Persia and the seven countries, and under his sway were a hundred princes, sitting on chairs of red gold, and ten thousand brave captains, armed with sword and ax. But the Sultan was at the point of death. They found him lying on his bed, with his face wrapped in bandages, groaning with pain.

Hassib kissed the ground before the Sultan, and prayed

for the blessing of Allah upon him. Then the Wazir seated Hassib on a chair of state at the Sultan's right hand, and he said to Hassib, "We are all your servants. We will give you anything you ask, even half the kingdom, if you will cure the Sultan."

Hassib answered, "It is true, O Wazir, that I am the son of Daniel, who was a prophet of Allah and a great healer, but I know nothing of his art. They put me for thirty days in the school of medicine and I learned nothing. I cannot heal the Sultan."

"Do not put us off with idle words," replied the Wazir sternly. "It is written that the remedy for the Sultan is with the Queen of the Serpents, and you know where she is to be found, for you have been with her."

Hassib was terrified. "No," he cried, "I don't know her. I've never heard of her."

"You lie to us," said the Wazir, even more sternly. "I have proof that you have spent two years with her."

He took a scroll from a servant, and unrolled it, and read, "The Queen of the Serpents shall meet a man, a son of Daniel, who shall remain with her for two years. Then he shall return to the surface of the earth, and when he enters the hammam his belly shall turn black." Then he added, "Look at your belly."

Hassib uncovered his belly, and it was black. He cried out in dismay, "My belly has been black from my birth."

"Three servants of mine were watching all bathers in the hammam," replied the Wazir. "They saw that before you entered the bath your belly was not black. All we ask is that you show us the place where you came out of the country of the Queen of the Serpents. Then we can compel her to come to us."

Then the Wazir and all the great lords pleaded with Hassib for an hour to show them this place, but he said over and over again that he knew nothing of the Queen of the Serpents.

Then the Wazir called the Chief Executioner, who stripped Hassib of his robes of honor and beat him until at last he cried out in pain that he would show them the place.

At that they raised him to his feet, and bathed his wounds and put on him a robe of honor made of cloth of red gold embroidered with priceless jewels. They set him on one of the Sultan's finest horses and he led them to the cave. There they gathered around the pit which had contained the honey. Servants brought the Wazir a charcoal brazier and lit it. The Wazir scattered on it magic herbs from which there rose a great smoke, while he uttered secret and terrible words of power, for he was a cunning magician.

Then he cried three times, "Come forth, O Queen of the Serpents, come forth!"

At the third time there was a roll of thunder so terrifying that they all fell prostrate on the earth, thinking their last hour had come. Then the Queen rose from the pit. She was coiled in a great golden dish, borne up by a gigantic serpent, which cast fiery sparks from its eyes and mouth. Beside the Queen in the dish lay three phials. The radiant splendor of her shining serpent body filled the cave with light, but her beautiful face was dark with anger.

She looked right and she looked left until she saw the Wazir. "O man of evil," she cried, "if I blew upon you there would be nothing left of you but a little heap of ashes. But it is written that your cruel magic shall master me. In token of your mastery take the silver phial which lies beside me." He took it with trembling hands and prostrated himself. "That phial," she said, "contains the liquor of life. Drink it after the Sultan has been healed, but not before. Drink it then and you shall never suffer from any human ailment again."

She looked right and she looked left; she looked at Hassib, and she said, "O Hassib, you have broken your oath to me, but I know you were forced into the hammam and you were almost beaten to death before you betrayed me. It was the will of Allah. You have my forgiveness. Take the two phials which are beside me."

He answered, "To hear is to obey," and took them.

"The golden phial is for you," she said. "You must drink it as soon as you reach the palace. The phial of emerald contains the liquor of healing, which will make the Sultan whole."

She looked again at the Wazir and cried, "It is finished. Let me go!"

The Wazir, trembling before her, lifted both arms and made a strange sign in the air. There was a roll of thunder even more terrible than the first and she was gone.

Then they rode to the palace, and on the threshold Hassib drank the liquor from the golden phial, which was indeed the liquor of wisdom. He looked up and saw the seven heavens, and understood the workings of the stars. He looked down and saw all the minerals and treasures which are hidden in the earth. He looked about him, and saw into the hearts and minds of men.

Then he went in to the Sultan and gave him the liquor of healing to drink. The Sultan slept for seven hours, and when he awoke all the leprosy was gone; he was healthier than he had been when the disease first took hold of him. The Wazir and all the princes and courtiers gathered to give him joy of his recovery. They beat the drums and decorated the city with flags and flowers.

Then the Wazir drank the liquor from the silver phial. It dropped from his hands and a moment later he fell dead. He had no more ailments, as the Queen had promised him.

The Sultan mourned the death of his Wazir, but he set Hassib beside him on the throne, and they ate and drank and talked much together, and the Sultan saw Hassib's wisdom. So he called together all the princes and great lords and captains of his kingdom, and said to them, "This is Hassib Karim al-Din, who has saved my life and is full of wisdom. I make him my Grand Wazir; whoever honors him, honors me; whoever obeys him, obeys me."

All the grandees kissed Hassib's hands in homage. The Sultan heaped wealth and honors on him, and he served the Sultan faithfully all his life. He lived happily with his wife and mother and was honored by everyone as the wisest man in the Sultan Karazdan's kingdom.

About the Author

JOHN HAMPDEN has written a number of books for young people, among them *The Gypsy Fiddle and Other Tales Told by the Gypsies* (World), a collection which reflects his life-long interest in folklore. Mr. Hampden is British, and lives in Sussex, England.

About the Artist

KURT WERTH is one of America's best-known illustrators. He was born in Germany and received his art training there, but he is now an American citizen, living in New York City.